THE CRITICS LOVE MAMA!

"Grace, aka Mama, Covington. . . . [is] a fabulous cook and a canny sleuth."
—*Booknews* from The Poisoned Pen

"A woman's voice—specifically Mama's—is clearly heard and answered in the mystery novels of Nora DeLoach."
—*American Visions* magazine

"Mama is an adorable detective, who readers will love for her southern grace, kindness, and charity. Nora DeLoach captures the essence of small town life . . . just like a Jessica Fletcher story."
—*Midwest Book Review*

"Grace Covington [has been] dubbed the African-American Miss Marple."
—*The San Diego Union-Tribune*

"Southern honesty and grit."
—*Chicago Tribune*

"African American Nora DeLoach has staked out the cozy southern territory with her series about 'Mama.' "
—*Feminist Bookstore News*

"[An] amusing yet solid series that revolves around a close-knit African-American family . . . Mama and Simone are a winsome pair of sleuths, affectionate in their relationship and respectful of each other's intellige   complements her
scenes of
—*Sun-Sent*

Also by Nora DeLoach

MAMA ROCKS THE EMPTY CRADLE
MAMA STALKS THE PAST

BJ—

Mama Pursues Murderous Shadows

Nora DeLoach

NORA DeLOACH

BANTAM BOOKS

NEW YORK TORONTO LONDON

SYDNEY AUCKLAND

MAMA PURSUES MURDEROUS SHADOWS
A Bantam Book / June 2000

ISBN 0-553-57722-0

Published simultaneously in the United States and Canada

Bantam Books are published by Bantam Books, a division of
Random House, Inc. Its trademark, consisting of the words
"Bantam Books" and the portrayal of a rooster, is Registered in
U.S. Patent and Trademark Office and in other countries. Marca
Registrada. Bantam Books, 1540 Broadway, New York, New York
10036.

PRINTED IN THE UNITED STATES OF AMERICA

OPM   10 9 8 7 6 5 4 3 2 1

ACKNOWLEDGMENTS

Thanks to the many readers who contacted me to share their delight in becoming acquainted with Mama. I am pleased so many people enjoy visiting Mama (Candi), Simone, James, Cliff, and their family and friends in Otis, South Carolina. My sincere desire is that Mama will continue to provide her fans with years of delightful and intriguing mysteries.

Mama Pursues
Murderous Shadows

PROLOGUE

Ruby Spikes bolted straight up and opened her eyes. Sweat rolled off her body like it was near a furnace—her ivory nightgown stuck to her skin like glue. Her heart pounded, her lungs felt about to burst.

She was in bed at the Avondale Inn. She tried to gain control but the memory of the excruciating nightmare gripped her remorselessly. The dream had been so real: *Everything was bright! Things were going to work out. Toward what she somehow knew was the east, a dark cloud hovered. Then, suddenly the light vanished. Rain, lightning, and thunder cracked all around her. A small house, no bigger than the box that her refrigerator had been delivered in, stood in the darkness in front of her. Its door opened and she rushed inside.*

She felt safe.

Then she saw the water on the floor. The little house was flooding. Desperate, she tried to open the door. It was locked.

Glad that she had awakened, she stared around the room. It was decorated in blue and white with a bordered wallpaper of a textured red. The tangled bedspread was patterned in red, white, and blue checks.

To the right was a closet. Across from the closet was a dressing area with a mirrored vanity and sink. Next to it, a door led to a toilet, a shower, towels. Instead of hanging up her clothes, she'd thrown her outfit on the upholstered blue chair next to the door.

On one nightstand was a telephone, a clock radio, and the remote control for the television; on the other, the neatly stacked and counted two thousand dollars she'd withdrawn from the bank.

She glanced at the clock. Midnight. Tears welled up in her eyes; aloneness carved another notch in her soul. Her life was a void, an emptiness that made her ask herself, *What is so wrong with me that nobody can love me?*

She looked at the money again. She was so tired. This would be the last time, she thought. It would take what little strength she had left, but if she could pull it off, she'd be free.

Ruby slipped out of bed and walked to the sink. She'd already taken all the pills she could safely take. For a moment she looked at herself in the mirror and wondered if she could really get away from the people of Otis and Avondale who had used and abused her.

The knock was so faint she thought at first that she'd imagined it. Silently, she eased toward the door.

"Ruby, let me in," a voice whispered.

The hopelessness she'd felt in her dream swept over her.

"Let me in," the voice pleaded again.

A warning inside of her head screamed not to open the door. She was so tired, so weak—she just couldn't fight any more. Ignoring the warning, she heaved a weary sigh and slipped the dead bolt from the door.

OTIS SHOOTING DEATH

The Otis Sheriff Department responded yesterday to a death at the Avondale Inn in Avondale, South Carolina. Coroner Robert Gordon said Ruby Jane Spikes, 26, of Otis, died of what appeared to be a self-inflicted gunshot wound to the chest. She was found by the maid at the Avondale Inn at around 9:00 Saturday morning. Spikes had checked into the room at 8:00 the previous night, according to Jeff Golick, the motel manager.

Officials do not suspect foul play. Spikes's body has been sent to the Charleston Medical Center for a routine autopsy.

Ruby Spikes was the wife of Herman Spikes of Otis.

CHAPTER
ONE

I was on a mission.

It was dark, rainy; a dreary dawn. I felt like it was only three A.M. and I owed my body another four hours' sleep. But the clock on the dashboard read six-thirty. I made a left, heading south onto Highway 20 off Wesley Chapel. I was driving to Otis, South Carolina, to visit my parents.

My mama, whose name is Grace but who is called Candi because of her golden-brown complexion, had firmly declined the suggestion of my brothers and me to throw her and my father a wedding anniversary party. It was their thirty-fifth, their jade anniversary, and my mission on this last Saturday in July was to change her mind!

"James and I don't need a party to celebrate our togetherness," Mama had informed me firmly when

I told her of our plans in a recent telephone conversation. "We do that every day."

"Mama," I'd replied, trying not to sound exasperated by her reluctance, "you and Daddy celebrate every day, but your *children* want to celebrate the thirty-fifth year of your marriage with both of you!"

Mama's voice brightened. "Then come home and I'll cook."

"We don't want you to cook!"

I'd said the wrong thing. . . . There was a dead silence.

"Mama," I explained hastily, "I'm not saying that we don't want you to cook for us. You and I know that most people who've tasted your cooking would crawl on their hands and knees to get just a morsel of—"

"Simone, you're exaggerating," Mama interrupted.

"Mama, we want to do something *special* for you and Daddy on your anniversary," I persisted. My mother isn't the only stubborn one in the family. "You're always doing things for us."

"Like what?"

"Like cooking," I said, hoping to convey that we knew that she was doing something *very* special whenever she cooked for her family.

"I don't like parties," Mama snapped.

I decided to ignore her tone. "I'll get Yasmine to help. My girlfriend is not only one of the best beauticians in Atlanta, but she also throws fabulous parties after hair and fashion shows. And, honest, Mama, Yasmine's got a real flare for—"

"Simone, I said *no*," Mama cut in.

"Will and Rodney want to come home to throw this party for you, Mama," I continued, knowing that using her sons as bait was one way to at least get her attention. That's not to say that Mama thinks more of her two boys than she does of me; I've never once felt that way. It's just that my brothers don't go back to Otis as much as Mama would like, and a visit from all three of her children at the same time is something that *really* turns her on.

"No." Mama's tone told me that she knew exactly what I was trying to do—I guess I'd used that technique too many times before.

"Okay," I said, deciding to switch gears. No matter her objections, I wasn't about to give in to her on this. You see, I work in the law office of Sidney Jacoby, a prominent Atlanta defense attorney. I'm a paralegal in the Research Department. My job requires me to grab onto a tiny bit of information that Sidney has unearthed and pursue it further. Usually, I'm like a pit bull, not letting go until I come up with something that Sidney can use. I guess what I'm saying is, I *know* how to be persistent. Most of the time, though, I don't try this routine with Mama—that's because most of the time I know that no matter how much time I put in trying to get her to change her mind, Mama's wishes always prevail.

On the subject of this anniversary party, however,

I was as determined as my mother can be when she makes her mind up. I'd already told Cliff, my boyfriend, a divorce lawyer who is on a partnership track in his law firm, that we were going to give Mama and Daddy the best anniversary party Otis had ever seen. "I'll make a deal with you," I now said to Mama in a more compromising tone.

"No deals, Simone," Mama said. *Her* tone didn't change.

I took a breath. "Mama, let me at least tell you what I had in mind."

"Why should I?"

"Because you're an open-minded woman," I said as sweet as I could.

Whether Mama fell for it or not, she said, "Go ahead."

I smiled, thinking I'd inched a little closer to convincing her. "If you let us have a party for you and Daddy," I wheedled, "I'll let you—"

Mama pounced. "You'll *let* me!"

"I mean"—I hastily changed my wording—"you can make *all* the arrangements. That way, the party will be just the way you like it."

"Simone, I don't—"

"Let me finish," I urged, taking advantage of the fact that her tone had become softer.

A sigh. "Go ahead."

"You'll pick the person who will do the cooking and someone to do the baking. I know you won't find anybody who's as good of a cook as you are, but at least you'll know that the food is acceptable."

Silence.

"Think about it," I added quickly, praying her silence suggested that I'd pried open a tiny possibility. "I'll come home on Saturday. We'll talk about it then, okay?"

"If you insist." She still sounded unconvinced. "But—"

"The party will be wonderful, exactly the way you want it to be," I promised. "There will be *no* surprises."

"What time can I expect you to come in on Saturday morning?"

"Around ten-thirty."

"That's late for breakfast."

"Save mine," I said.

"James is going to North Carolina on an all-day fishing trip," she said.

"Then it'll be a good day for us to spend together," I told her. "Just the two of us. Mama, I love you," I added.

"Love you too," Mama replied before she hung up, her voice sunnier now that she knew that I was coming home again.

My father retired as a captain from the United States Air Force after thirty years of service. During that time, he and my mother parented two boys— Will and Rodney—and me—Simone. My brothers and I were fortunate in that we lived in five different countries while growing up.

9

When Daddy decided to retire, Mama and I shared the thought that it wasn't right for them to move back to Otis, Daddy and Mama's hometown. After all, Otis barely has five thousand people living in it. And those people are far from being cosmopolitan—most of them have never lived any other place. A few of them have never been two hundred miles northwest to Atlanta.

Otis used to be a town of soybeans, watermelons, and cotton fields. Large tracts of land in the surrounding county are owned by families like ours who, at Reconstruction, when the government gave each freed slave forty acres and a mule, got their first taste of land ownership. About ten years ago, a company started buying the land when older members of those families died out, moved away, or didn't pay their taxes. That company now owns 2,500 acres. They tree-farm the land, and they, along with other farmers who decided to stop farming and plant trees, keep loggers and the Otis Sawmill busy most all year around.

My parents live in a brick ranch house on a one-acre lot on Smalls Lane. Their front yard has two sprawling magnolia trees. My father was wise enough not to allow the old trees to be cut down when he had the house built. Last year they remodeled the back of the house so that their kitchen and family room, with floor-to-ceiling windows, open into a backyard garden. One large oak sits in the center of the yard. Roses, azaleas, and annuals border a chain-link fence. Daddy's dog, Midnight, has access to the backyard through a gate that's never locked.

Smalls Lane is a cul-de-sac; my parents' house shares the street with four other homes. It was there I was headed.

"Sarah Jenkins has been admitted to Otis General."

That's how Mama greeted me when I walked into her home ready to do more battle with her about her anniversary party.

Sarah Jenkins, along with Annie Mae Gregory and Carrie Smalls, are the town's gossips. I call them Otis's historians because these three women know everything about everybody. Mama, however, refers to them as her "sources." That's because Sarah, Annie Mae, and Carrie have told her things that have helped her solve various cases in town. Let me explain—Mama was bitten by the sleuthing bug when I was a little girl. When one of her neighbors told her something that didn't sit just right with her, she couldn't rest until she tracked down the tale and found the truth. Since that time, Mama has to find the truth; she sees it as her contribution to her community.

Sarah Jenkins is a tiny, frail-looking woman with a wrinkled, pecan-colored complexion. She spends as much time in the doctor's office as he does. So I wasn't surprised to hear that she was in the hospital.

"Sarah's just having a reaction to some of the many medications the doctor is giving her," I told Mama as I sat down in front of three fat golden-brown slices of French toast. On the table was a jug of maple syrup, diced cantaloupe, apple juice, and an Ethiopian blend of coffee that Mama gets me to send her from the Caribou Coffee Shop on Peachtree Street in Atlanta's Buckhead district.

Mama looked doubtful. "Gertrude didn't say what's ailing Sarah," she replied, shaking her head.

Gertrude Covington is Daddy's first cousin; she works at the hospital as a nurse's aide, a job Gertrude loves because she gets to know who goes in and out of the hospital.

"Listen, lady," I told Mama, wagging my fork in the air, "you and I need to talk about your party, remember? After all, that's the reason I came all the way home this weekend. Finding out which one of Sarah's many complaints sent her running to the hospital is just not our priority this visit, okay?"

Mama's look stayed stubborn. "I was thinking," she said, "of Barbara Fleming."

I waited.

"Barbara is a fairly good baker—she'd be the perfect person to do the baking," Mama continued.

"You mean you're going to let us throw you and Daddy the party!" I exclaimed, astonished.

"Are you going to let me get away with *not* having it?" Mama asked.

I got up, scooted around the table, and hugged

her. "Not this time, pretty lady, and you're going to love what I have in mind—"

Mama pulled back, surprised. "I thought *I* would be the one to make the decisions on how this party will be handled," she said.

"Uh, yes—"

"Go back and finish your breakfast," she said.

I obeyed.

"Now," she continued, "I've decided that the party will be held here in Otis at the Community Center."

I nodded; my mouth was too full of French toast for me to speak.

"I'll make up the guest list, plan the menu, and—"

"I know," I said, now that I'd swallowed. "You'll hire the caterer!"

Mama's eyebrows raised. "You've got a problem with that?"

"I was just wondering whether you're going to let me do *anything*."

The warm, glowing smile that tells me that I will always be a part of whatever she does flashed across Mama's face. "Truth is, I was thinking that it would be nice if you and your friend Yasmine took care of the flowers, the decorations, and picking out invitations."

"I got you," I said, finishing up my French toast and reaching for the cantaloupe. "James and Candi's anniversary bash is going to be the biggest thing this town has ever seen."

"It'll be a nice party," Mama agreed, so low that you'd almost think she was talking to herself. "I've got to think of letting Gertrude and Agatha do something to help."

I've already told you about Daddy's cousin Gertrude, but he's got another cousin who's very important to the Covington family. Her name is Agatha; she's a spinster who manages the family heirs' property—the hundreds of acres of land that my great-grandfather amassed when his fellow freed slaves deeded him their forty acres and decided to migrate north.

Mama sat straight up in her chair. "First thing we've got to do as soon as you finish eating, Simone, is go to the hospital and visit Sarah Jenkins."

CHAPTER
TWO

Otis County General Hospital, like all hospitals, is a sanctuary—a sterile place that smells of medicines and powerful disinfectants. It's supposed to be a haven for the sick and injured. You'd think Sarah Jenkins would feel right at home in such a place, since she's *enjoyed* so many infirmities and ailments over the years.

Today, though, it was clear that Sarah wasn't having fun.

Mama, who is normally composed under most circumstances, couldn't hold back her astonishment. "My Lord, Sarah, what's wrong? What happened?"

Sarah was sitting up in bed, and although I was sure she'd been given at least a mild sedative, her coal black eyes were as large as silver dollars. Tears sparkled in them. Her trembling hands clutched the neck of her pale blue hospital garment as if she was

15

holding the gown closed to keep somebody from snatching it from her. I don't know if it was because of whatever medication she had been given or her mental state, but sweat formed like little pearl beads on her forehead. "Candi," she gasped, her voice desperate, her eyes frantic, "thank God you've finally come!"

I glanced at Sarah's two constant companions. Annie Mae Gregory is a very fat, very dark woman with eyes that are small and very piercing. Set deep in her fat face, Annie Mae's eyes always remind me of a raccoon's—bright and extremely inquisitive. When her head is tilted a certain way, she looks cross-eyed.

Carrie Smalls, on the other hand, is tall, with mocha skin and straight, shoulder-length hair. Carrie looks younger than her two friends but that's because she dyes her hair jet black. She also has a strong chin, thin lips, and eyes that seldom seem to blink. She has a scary strength about her. I always tell Mama that it's Carrie Smalls's strength that gives these three women their presence when they're together.

Sarah's two companions sat on chairs on each side of her hospital bed, arms folded over their bosoms like they were Roman sentries standing guard at their post. Carrie's back was so straight you'd think she's carried books on her head most of her life. "Pull up a chair," she told Mama in a tone that sounded like a command.

Mama complied. I stood behind Mama's chair.

"Candi," Sarah wailed, gripping her hospital gown. *"You've got to help me!"*

Mama reached over and patted Sarah's arm. "I'll do what I can," she soothed. "But, Sarah, tell me exactly what's happened."

"You heard that Ruby Spikes was found dead in one of the rooms at the Avondale Inn, haven't you?"

Mama nodded.

"Ruby was my godchild, Candi. After her mama and daddy died, I took out a life insurance policy on her. I've paid one dollar and fifty cents a week for the past ten years."

Before Sarah had a chance to finish her story Carrie Smalls blurted out, "The insurance company won't pay Sarah the five-thousand-dollar face value of the policy. Sarah almost had a heart attack when she found out that she wasn't going to get her hands on that money. That's why she's here!"

"It ain't right," Sarah said dramatically. "Carrie and Annie Mae know I paid my premiums regularly!"

Annie Mae spoke for the first time, her fat body shaking like Jell-O. "That's right. I can testify to the fact that Bobby Campbell shows up on Sarah's doorstep every Monday morning to collect that money."

Mama took a deep breath. "The only thing I can suggest is that you report this to Abe," she offered. Abe Stanley is Otis's sheriff.

Sarah Jenkins clutched her nightgown even

tighter. "I've gone to Abe," she wailed. "He claims there ain't nothing he can do to make Bobby pay the policy."

"I don't believe him," Carrie Smalls interjected sternly.

"Why won't Bobby pay the policy?" I asked, not understanding why she couldn't get the money.

Sarah cut her eyes at me. "Bobby Campbell says that Ruby died by her own hands. And the insurance company won't pay in the case of suicide. But I know for a fact, Ruby wasn't about to kill herself!"

Carrie leaned forward. "I was in Capers Hardware two days before Ruby died. I heard her order a brand new washer and dryer from old man Capers. Candi, do you think Ruby would have ordered that kind of thing and then decide to kill herself?"

The light in Mama's eyes as she sat there thinking was the glint that always shines in them when her sleuthing instinct is aroused. I was a bit concerned. I could tell that Sarah's plea had struck a chord with Mama, and I didn't want her tied up with Ruby Spikes's suicide, apparent or otherwise—I wanted her to help me plan her party!

"The paper is lying, Bobby Campbell is lying, Abe—" Sarah sounded absolutely frantic.

"Sarah, I really don't see that there is anything I can do," Mama said, getting to her feet.

I let out a breath, one that I didn't know I was holding. Mama appeared to have shaken off the inclination to dig into Ruby's death, and I was glad!

18

But Sarah grabbed for Mama's hand. "Candi," she pleaded, "you've got to help me. . . . I *need* that five thousand dollars." She hesitated. "I need it to pay my property taxes." Now she looked ashamed, like a small child who had just been caught stealing. "You see—"

"Sarah did a foolish thing—she used the money she'd saved to pay her taxes to play a lottery that a man sold her over the telephone," Carrie interrupted.

Sarah sat up straight in her hospital bed. "The nice young man talked so sweet. You'd have believed him, too."

The glint in Mama's eyes I dreaded so much was back. She was interested in this drama that I was sure Sarah was playing out just to get her all tangled up in Ruby's death. "What did he promise you?" she asked Sarah gently.

"He told me that I'd already won three times what I needed to pay my taxes. I just knew the Lord had heard my prayers and sent me a blessing."

Mama looked surprised. "You sent your tax money to a stranger simply because he told you you'd won the lottery?"

"There was more to it than that, Candi," Sarah tried to explain. "You see, the first thing I got was this notice in the mail that said I'd won the lottery in Canada. Just a few days after that, I got this call from a very nice young man. He explained to me that I'd won the money, that it was mine fair and square.

He told me that all I needed to do to get the check was to send him fifteen hundred dollars for the paperwork."

"And you sent it!" I exclaimed, incredulous.

"Over six weeks ago," Sarah confessed. "I ain't heard a word since then and I don't have no way of getting in touch with the young man I talked to over the phone."

"No telephone number? What about an address?"

"The only thing I've got is this letter." Sarah pulled a crumpled paper from under her pillow and handed it to Mama. I read it over Mama's shoulder, and my heart sank. It was the standard swindle letter, promising big winnings. Sarah started to cry. "Candi, I sent him my tax money. If I don't pay my taxes by the end of August, I'll lose my place. So naturally when I heard that poor Ruby had died, I remembered that I had this little policy that I'd been paying on since she was sixteen, so I called Bobby Campbell. Candi, I've got to get that money," she sobbed. "I'll lose my place, my home. I'll lose everything I own!"

"Sarah's heart couldn't take the strain of the thought of losing her place," Annie Mae told Mama. "She carried on so last night, it took two doctors and three nurses just to try to calm her nerves."

"Promise me you'll prove that Ruby didn't kill herself, that somebody killed her," Sarah begged my mother as she hung on to Mama's arm like the hospital bed was the *Titanic* and she was about to sink under icy waters.

Empathy swept across Mama's face, and to be honest, I didn't like the look. You see, Mama is a caseworker at the county's Department of Social Services. She enjoys fitting together the puzzle pieces of other people's lives, and she becomes positively euphoric when her mind is deducing.

The problem that faced Mama now was that Sarah Jenkins desperately needed money. Sarah could get that money if Ruby Spikes had not committed suicide but had been murdered. To me, there was no mystery: Ruby Spikes had killed herself, just like the coroner and the newspaper said. But the tone of Mama's voice when she spoke to Sarah Jenkins told me that she didn't share my conviction.

"I'll talk to Abe," Mama told Sarah kindly. "In the meantime, you rest." She patted Sarah's hand.

"If poor Ruby was murdered, you'd better hurry and find her killer," Carrie Smalls said as she stretched her thin neck and folded her hands tight under her bosom. "Monday, August thirtieth, is the last day to pay taxes. After that, Sarah's property will be posted in the *Otis County Guardian* as being up for sale. Everybody in the county will be talking about the people who didn't have sense enough to save money for their taxes!"

Sarah's eyes closed; her thin body shuddered.

"I know I wouldn't want my name published and my property in the paper," Carrie Smalls continued in her steely voice. "There are people in this county who wait for that yearly notice of taxes that haven't been paid. I reminded Sarah and she knows I ain't lying. As soon as they see the names in that notice and they see it's property they've been wanting, they run to the courthouse, pay the back taxes, and, if nobody in the family shows up in a year's time, they get heirs' property for the unpaid taxes. The man that lives next door to Sarah has been trying to get her to sell her family land for the past few years. I wouldn't put it past him to be the first to the courthouse after that newspaper comes out!"

Carrie Smalls's observation did little to console her friend.

"Lord, please help, Candi! My great-granddaddy would turn over in his grave if he knew I lost the homestead for lack of paying taxes!" Sarah Jenkins wailed.

My heart sank.

Mama was sleuthing again.

CHAPTER
THREE

Abe Stanley has been the sheriff of Otis County for the past twenty-five years. He's a tall white man, with soft wispy gray hair at his temples. His long, narrow face has deep lines that express every nuance of whatever he feels. Abe is a three-pack-a-day smoker; there is always a cigarette in his mouth or hand.

Mama got to know Abe right after my father retired. This is how it happened: Mama, who has a degree in sociology from the University of the State of New York, landed a job as a case manager for Otis County Department of Social Services shortly after she and my father moved back to Otis.

One day while Mama was visiting one of her welfare clients, she got a flat tire. She was on a lonely stretch of Highway 3, five miles outside of Otis. Fortunately for Mama, Sheriff Abe and his deputy, Rick

Martin, were driving by. Abe stopped his car and had Rick change Mama's tire. Later that evening, Mama rewarded their kindness with a sweet-potato pie.

Anybody who has ever eaten even the smallest bite of Mama's pie, or anything else she's ever cooked, would understand why Abe immediately became so attached to my mother. I think Abe sees Mama as his Associate Sheriff, if there is such a thing.

Mama really loved the idea of becoming the sheriff's confidante. It gave her the opportunity to learn things about people who live in Otis, people she thought she knew but who turned out to be very different than the way she remembered them when she and Daddy first lived there, over thirty years ago, before Daddy joined the Air Force, and Rodney, Will, and I were born. She helped Abe solve several crimes by making suggestions that steered him in the right direction. She's helped him solve four different cases so far. Mama's assistance with Abe's law enforcement, as well as her gift for out-baking anybody who lives within a hundred-mile radius, really sealed the close relationship between her and the sheriff.

Her relationship with Rick Martin isn't the same. While Abe's face is expressive, Rick has that simple look that makes you wonder if he's operating one short of a six-pack. A young man who has never ventured to travel any further than the four surrounding counties, Rick shows little or no emotion. But he's not stupid, for he can hold up his end of a satisfying conversation, and he loves to talk whenever Mama and Abe give him a chance.

The front door of the Otis jail opens into a small foyer. On the left side, a door leads into a room that has one large desk, one small desk, two executive chairs, two file cabinets, an old water cooler, a small table with a coffee urn on it, and four wooden chairs. This is the domain of Sheriff Abe and his deputy.

On the other side of the foyer is a door that leads to three holding cells, residence for those who break Otis's laws.

"Abe," Mama began after a few minutes of polite conversation in the sheriff's office that very afternoon, "I've just come from the hospital visiting Sarah."

The lines in the sheriff's face deepened; he slouched in his chair. "I know she's in a terrible state," he said as he slipped the unlit cigarette from between his lips and dropped it on his desk because he respected Mama by never lighting up when she was around. "I've talked to Dr. Mark, the doctor who was on duty last night when Annie Mae and Carrie brought Sarah in. He told me that he only gave Sarah a mild sedative until he can get hold of Dr. Baker, her personal doctor. He needs to find out what other kinds of medications she's been taking for all those ailments she's been complaining of for years." He shook his head sorrowfully.

"Sarah foolishly got rid of her tax money," Mama said. "Now that her taxes are due, she's not able to pay them. I understand once she learned that poor

Ruby Spikes was dead, her hope was that she could collect from a policy that she'd been paying on Ruby for some years. But Bobby Campbell won't pay the policy because of the way Ruby died."

"I know Sarah's dilemma, Candi, but there ain't nothing I can do about it."

"Is there any indication that Ruby Spikes *didn't* commit suicide?" Mama asked Abe.

He shifted uneasily in his chair. "Candi, Ruby was sprawled in the middle of the floor, the gun in her hand. There was no sign of a struggle, no sign of breaking and entering. She was dressed in her night-gown; her medicine was lined up on the sink. Her pocketbook, her car keys, wallet, checkbook was all there just like they hadn't been touched. The bed did look as if she'd been in it for a while, but that's understandable since she was dressed for bed. Why Ruby got up that night and wrote this note"—he reached into a drawer and handed a sheet of white paper to Mama—"I can't for the life of me understand."

Mama read the note; her eyebrows rose. Then she passed it to me. It read: *Life ain't worth living. Ruby.*

"I compared the writing against the writing on the registration slip that Ruby filled out when she checked into the Inn," Abe continued. "Ruby wrote that note all right, and the only prints we found in the room belonged to the maid and Ruby."

"Still," Mama said to Abe, "the look on your face tells me that you've got concerns."

"My first concern is that her room door was unlocked. Why wouldn't she lock it before she shot herself? Second, the wound was downward, as if Ruby had been shot by someone taller than she was," Abe admitted. "But there is something that I didn't give to the newspapers that really bothers me. I found a piece of paper in Ruby's left hand that looks like the torn edge of a piece of money. I can't help but wonder why she was clutching the edge of a piece of money in her hand. And what happened to the rest of it? I've sent the paper to the lab. The only other unusual things in that motel room were tiny bits of rubber in the carpet, and a receipt from a certified check for five thousand dollars we found in Ruby's purse. That check was made out to a Charles Parker, and I don't know who Charles Parker is." He sighed and poked at his cigarette. "Well, Candi, you asked me, so I've told you my concerns. But my concerns are not enough to override the evidence that all points to Ruby having killed herself. . . .

"Poor Ruby," he continued grimly. "Seems like that girl was destined to meet her fate. Why, just a week ago, I got a call to go out to the Spikeses' house. It was on Saturday morning, a little after daylight. When I got there, Ruby was in a state—you'd think she'd wrestled with a ghost.

"Ruby's story was this: She was home alone—it seems that Herman, her old man, hadn't gotten in as yet. While Ruby was asleep, a man slipped into a window at the rear of the house, went to a closet in the hallway, and got a blanket. He threw the blanket over Ruby's head and then tried to rape her. She put up a terrific fight—I could see the bruises on her face, neck, and hands. Still, this fella wouldn't give up until he heard Herman's car drive up in the yard. It was only then that he turned Ruby loose and fled through the back window."

"How horrible," Mama murmured.

"It happens all the time in Atlanta," I said. Mama's glare told me that Otis wasn't Atlanta.

"Anyway," Abe continued, "I investigated. I got a piece of cloth that Ruby had torn from the intruder's shirt and a few smudged fingerprints on the window-sill and some skin samples that were taken from Ruby's fingernails. Don't think I've given up looking for that fella," he admitted with a heavy sigh. "To be truthful, Candi, I'm anxious to see what the pathologist at the medical center in Charleston finds when he performs the autopsy. I'm hoping that maybe he'll come up with something that will tie this intruder with Ruby's death. If that happens, I'll be looking for a rapist and maybe even a killer. Ruby's doctor told me that she was pretty torn up about the attempted rape. Her nerves were already bad; he'd prescribed some powerful sleeping medicine. He kind of suggested that knowing Ruby's mental state, he wasn't surprised that she killed herself after that attack."

"Then it doesn't look like Sarah is going to collect on Ruby's insurance policy," I said. To my mind, Ruby had obviously committed suicide, distraught over the terrible assault she had suffered in her own home just the week before her death.

Abe twisted in his swivel chair. "I sure can't ignore all that evidence just to support Sarah's contention that Ruby didn't kill herself," he told Mama, sounding regretful.

"It was foolish of Sarah to fall for that scam," Mama told him, "but I understand it's the kind of thing that happens too often to too many older citizens."

"It's a fact," Abe agreed. "But law enforcement in this country can't do much about a swindler in another country. I've known Sarah Jenkins most of my life, Candi, and I can't imagine why she'd send her hard-earned money to a complete stranger."

Mama shook her head sadly. "Sarah is convinced that Ruby didn't kill herself."

"I know," Abe said. "And she might be right, too. My gut feeling is that something went on in that motel room that we need to know before we can say for sure how Ruby died. Once I get the autopsy report, I may have something to work with. Until I get something more, though, I just don't have enough evidence to launch an official investigation." He looked into Mama's eyes. "Still, Candi, it won't do any harm for you to talk to folks about Ruby's death. If you learn something that would support Sarah's contention, I wouldn't frown on it if you shared it with me. . . ."

CHAPTER
FOUR

For days later, I got a phone call from Mama.

It was almost eight on a steamy hot August evening. I'd only been in my apartment for half an hour, long enough to have tried on the two skirts I'd just purchased. I had made a stop at the Macy's Wednesday sale, one of my favorite pastimes.

"Simone," Mama began immediately after her greeting. "I've just visited Abe. He got a call from TJ Cohen, the personnel manager at the plant where Ruby Spikes worked. TJ told Abe that he'd cleaned out Ruby's locker and found a notebook inside of it. Ruby kept a diary. She had been jotting down her feelings. Abe let me read the book. That poor woman was an emotional wreck. She wrote all about her turmoil, about her terrible marriage and how unloved she felt. And there were quite a few passages where she'd talked about being free from Otis, from

Avondale, and from the people who hurt her. Poor woman wanted desperately to find peace."

For a moment Mama's news fostered my hope that she would back away from trying to help Sarah out of her tax troubles. "That settles it, then," I said. "Ruby committed suicide and Sarah might as well accept the fact that she won't get any money from the insurance policy."

I could hear Mama sigh—this, for those of you who don't know Mama, was not a good sign. "I'm really worried about Sarah," she told me. "The whole town knows that she's lost her tax money to a scam. She told me that her neighbor, the one who had offered to buy her property, has already been looking around her place, like he's making plans to buy her property for taxes. And she's gotten several phone calls from people who buy land at a discount from people who are about to lose it for taxes. That poor woman is in such a state, this thing might be the death of her."

"Come on, Mama," I insisted. "Sarah is the victim of no one but her own greed. She got her own butt in a sling, so she deserves the pain! Besides, she's spent years gloating over other people's misfortune; it's payback time. What goes around comes around!"

"That doesn't make it easier for her," Mama responded.

"And she's been sickly all of her life. Falling for some lottery scam and losing her property won't be the only thing that will put her on her death—"

Mama cut in sternly. "Simone, there's no need for you to rub Sarah's faults in—she's worried sick."

Even though Mama couldn't see me, I rolled my eyes. "It's about time somebody rubs her faults in her face, since she's been throwing mud into other people's faces for years," I said angrily. "Sarah had no business sending her tax money to a con artist in Canada. If that had happened to somebody else in town, she'd taunt them to death!"

Mama shot back, "That's beside the point."

I wasn't getting the response I'd been hoping for. I knew by Mama's tone that she wanted to help Sarah. I tried to deflect that desire by harping on the fact that Sarah had willingly submitted to being swindled. "Mama, Sarah Jenkins *deserves* whatever happens to her. It's not your place to get involved in trying to help her!"

I expected that Mama would give me a jab back, telling me how judgmental I sounded in my assessment of how poor Sarah had gotten herself in dire financial difficulty. Instead, when she replied, there was nothing but concern in her voice. "I'm worried about Sarah's health and her taxes, of course, but the truth is, since Abe and I have talked again, I can't get past the fact that it's quite possible that poor Ruby didn't kill herself, and if that is the case—"

"If somebody killed Ruby, what could be their motive?" I demanded. "And how could they have done it? I was there when Abe told you that there were no fingerprints in the room except Ruby's and the maid's."

"I gave Sarah my word that I'd look into Ruby's death," Mama told me. "And you were with me when Abe encouraged me to talk to people about it!"

Now, at this point I should have been convinced that it would be useless for me to try to sway Mama. I knew all too well what I'd heard in her tone—her sleuthing instinct had been aroused by both Sarah's plight and Abe's concern. Still, I wasn't ready to accept the inevitable. "What about your party?" I asked, no doubt sounding overwhelmingly concerned about my own agenda.

Surprisingly, Mama seemed to understand. "What about it?"

"Are we still going for it?"

"Of course, Simone," she answered confidently. "I expected you'd be coming home this Saturday so that we can make further plans."

"Yes?" I said, encouraged.

"I'm looking forward to your coming," Mama said before she hung up.

I arrived in Otis about ten o'clock Saturday morning. My father, Abe, and Mama were sitting at the kitchen table. The sheriff was eating from a heaping plate of pancakes, sausage, and fluffy scrambled eggs. Daddy sipped from a cup of Colombian coffee whose rich aroma seemed to fill the room.

I'll bet this is Abe's second breakfast today, I thought as I poured myself a full cup of fragrant coffee. I looked at Mama and smiled.

"I've saved your breakfast, Simone," Mama told me. From the microwave, she pulled out a plate of food piled as high as Abe's.

"I tried to leave early enough to get here in time," I admitted.

"Candi's breakfast is good any time of day," Abe said, his mouth full of eggs.

Daddy nodded; he loves hearing people compliment Mama's cooking.

"Candi," Abe said to Mama between mouthfuls, "I'm sorry to have to tell you this, but I won't be getting the autopsy report on Ruby Spikes for another few weeks. Dr. Sanford, the only certified pathologist at the medical center who handles autopsies for this part of the state, had an accident. His car hit a tree in a rainstorm and he injured his neck. It looks like I won't be able to do anything to change the cause of Ruby's death until Sanford's able to get back on the job and take care of that autopsy."

Mama looked at Abe. "I know you haven't set up a full investigation, but have you done anything about locating Charles Parker, the man Ruby gave that five-thousand-dollar certified check to?"

"I've told Rick to ask around town whether anybody knows the fella or not."

My father stood up and rolled his shoulders. "Candi baby, why are you so interested in Charles Parker? If Ruby gave this Parker money, I bet my week's pay that it will be one more thing that people will tease her husband Herman about. People have been on his case so hard, around Joe's Pool Hall, Herman is treated like a plucked chicken. I know he's embarrassed; he tries to act like it doesn't bother him by talking bad about Ruby. One day a few weeks ago he was so scornful I told my buddy Coal that Ruby would be better off without him. I didn't mean for her to go off and kill herself just to get rid of him, though," he muttered, shaking his head.

CHAPTER

FIVE

I turned the key in the ignition. Mama reached out and touched my arm. "Watch out for my neighbor's cat," she warned. "That animal loves to sleep under cars." Seconds later I flinched as a furry ball of orange and white darted out from under the wheels and across our front yard. Mama sighed with relief.

Once out on Smalls Lane, I made a left. Barbara Fleming, the woman Mama had decided would do the baking for her party, lived in Masonville, a town fifteen miles east of Otis.

When I turned into Barbara Fleming's driveway, I checked the clock on the dashboard. It was two o'clock.

Barbara's house was a traditional southern cottage on an oak-lined street. When this short, thin woman opened the door to us, we were ushered into an arched opening flanked by built-in bookcases.

The house had a pleasant scent, a mixture of lavender and rosemary.

Barbara Fleming had beautiful large, dark eyes with long lashes that accentuated her yellow complexion. She wore a denim dress that buttoned down the front.

We sat at the table in the all-white breakfast room making conversation as Barbara served coffee and rum-glazed banana cake. The cake was delicious, but not as good as the one Mama makes.

After we'd eaten, I stirred my second cup of coffee, feeling a twinge of impatience. Mama chattered on. I wanted her to start talking about the reason we'd come. She's hedging, I thought. My mama doesn't want to admit that somebody else's baking might suffice for her party.

Barbara was the one who finally brought the conversation to our purpose. "Candi," she said, "did I understand you to say when you telephoned that you want *me* to do the baking for a party?"

Mama nodded politely. "Simone and my boys insist on throwing me and James this anniversary party—"

"It's their thirty-fifth," I interrupted.

Mama went on, "Simone doesn't think it proper that I do the baking for this party, so—"

It was Barbara who interrupted this time. "Simone, do you think the flour, butter, and sugar I throw together will be anything like what your mama bakes?" she demanded.

Mama looked surprised. "You're a good cook,"

she told Barbara. "I've heard more than one person in town give you proper credit."

Barbara laughed stiffly. "The closest thing I ever get to a compliment about my cooking is that it's a good second to yours, Candi."

Mama shifted in her seat. "That's just not true," she said, clearly embarrassed.

"Barbara, if you do the baking," I chimed in, to move the conversation along toward the road I needed it to travel, "you won't have to compete with Mama on this one."

Barbara's thin shoulders relaxed. "Since you don't bake for a living, Candi, I get more than enough people asking me to bake for their special occasions." She smiled. "Well, what did you have in mind?"

Mama pulled out a list from her purse. "I'd like one hundred coconut cream puffs, three chocolate pound cakes, two orange cakes, three coconut-lemon cakes, six pecan pies, six apple pies, six sweet-potato pies, five butter pound cakes, and two hundred homemade butter crescent rolls."

From the expression on her face, it was clear Barbara Fleming didn't expect such a long list. She was staring at Mama.

"What about cheesecake?" I asked Mama sarcastically.

"Barbara, do you have a good cheesecake recipe?"

"I was only kidding," I said hastily.

But Barbara's look stayed serious. "That's a tall order, Candi," she pointed out.

For a second, I felt panic. If Barbara didn't agree to do the baking, Mama might not think anyone else in the county was good enough to do it. "The party is five weeks from now," I told her. As Mama was reading from her list, I couldn't help but wonder whether or not she purposefully made it so extensive in order that Barbara wouldn't be able to do it all. That would give Mama an excuse to pitch in and do some of the baking herself, something I was determined not to let happen.

Barbara walked over to a small desk, reached in, and pulled out a calendar. She flipped its pages and asked, "September fifteenth?"

"That's the date," I said.

"September fifteenth, from six to ten," Mama said.

Barbara raised an eyebrow. "Like I said, Candi," she began uncertainly, "it's a tall order . . . but I reckon I can pull that together for you."

I breathed a very loud sigh of relief, and Mama shot me a reproving look. "Now that *that* is settled, let's talk dollars and cents," I said, firmly signaling Mama to get lost for a few minutes. My brothers and I had agreed to foot all the bills for this party—we'd already determined a maximum spending limit.

Mama, as usual, instantly picked up on my look. She set her list down on the table, stood up, and looked around the room. "You have such a colorful backyard," she said.

Barbara's dark eyes lit up with pleasure. "It's going to be a garden whenever I get it finished," she murmured. "Right now, I call it my work in progress." She laughed.

"May I take a look?" Mama asked.

"Be my guest," Barbara said warmly. You could see that Mama's interest in her flowerbeds had finally thawed her chilly manner. "Just remember that it will look much better once it's finished."

Mama smiled and eased out through the door into the little backyard.

CHAPTER
SIX

"Now that we've made arrangements for the baking," Mama said, once we were seated in the Honda again, "drive me to Avondale. I had Abe call Jeff Golick, the manager of the Avondale Inn, to arrange for us to talk to him in about ten minutes, so please hurry!"

The town of Avondale, South Carolina, rises up like an oasis at the end of a twenty-mile drive on a two-lane highway, bordered by shallow ditches that run through a thickly planted pine tree farm. Although smaller than the town of Otis, Avondale has four motels, a Starvin Marvin, an Exxon, and a Chevron service station. It also boasts a liquor store, a McDonald's, a Hardee's, and a Huddle House restaurant. Avondale flanks an interstate that takes easterners into Florida.

The Avondale Inn has a cream-colored exterior with black trim and a look that tries too hard to be colonial. There were only three cars in the parking lot. As we walked inside, we spotted a man standing in the lobby outside the manager's office, pacing anxiously, repeatedly checking his watch. He had a pointed chin, a sharp nose, and dark, bushy eyebrows. The fat young clerk behind the counter stared at us like she knew her boss was very annoyed with us already.

"Mr. Golick?" Mama asked as we approached.

"Yes." The man's eyes darted toward us disapprovingly.

"Grace Covington," Mama told him. "And my daughter, Simone."

"I expected you five minutes ago," the manager snapped.

"It was nice of you to agree to talk with us," Mama continued, her voice low and pleasant.

"The sheriff told me to talk to you," Jeff Golick said, making it clear he would have preferred not to. "I don't understand what you have to do with Ruby killing herself. You can't be a friend. If I was a betting man, I'd put my money on the fact that Ruby didn't have any friends," he snarled.

"Why would you say that?" Mama asked.

"The only time that—" He stopped. "Look—Let's go into my office." He turned and led us into a large room in which there was a desk with an expensive computer. Jeff Golick sat behind the desk; Mama and I sat in the two very comfortable chairs that faced him. He sighed and spread his hands wide. "I'm not surprised Ruby killed herself."

Mama's eyebrows rose, but she said nothing.

"Ruby spent quite a few nights here, so I got to know her well. She always came for one of two reasons: Most of the time, it was because she'd had a fight with her husband and needed to get away for a night or two. If that girl had anyone to help her, she'd have gone to them when that goon started beating up on her. But she always came here," he said impatiently.

Mama nodded. "You said there was another reason that Ruby checked into your inn."

"She came to meet her . . . friend."

"Do you know Ruby's friend's name?" Mama asked quietly.

Golick shook his head. "I've only seen the man a few times as he slipped in and out of her room. I couldn't tell who he was."

Mama nodded again. "Tell me something about the last time that Ruby checked into the motel. Was her friend with her that night?"

"Friday night before—" His voice broke. "The Friday night before Ruby died," he continued gruffly, "my gut feeling was that she wasn't checking in to meet her friend."

"What made you think not?" Mama asked.

"Ruby's eyes were puffy like she'd been crying. I suppose if I had given it some thought, I should have known she'd try to hurt herself. The woman looked like she'd just thrown on her clothes without thinking, just to get away from whatever it was that was chasing her. I mean, it was a hot night and she was all bundled up in a thick black sweater and a scarf."

"A scarf?" Mama asked as she took out a small notebook from her purse and began making notes.

"Yeah, a reddish brown scarf that struck me as being particularly ugly," he replied.

"What did Ruby say to you?"

Jeff shifted in his chair. "Nothing, not a word, but like I told Abe, she had a good bit of money on her. When she opened her purse to pay for the room, I saw a roll big enough to choke a cow!"

Mama seemed to ponder what she'd just learned. "I was wondering why it was you that checked Ruby into the motel that night and not your front desk clerk."

"It was Maria's dinner hour," Jeff said, looking surprised. "Maria is my clerk. I always take care of the check-ins between eight and nine o'clock."

"Were there many people staying here that night?"

"It was a slow night. Just a trucker who stays here from time to time and an old couple from New York on their way to Miami."

Mama smiled appreciatively. "I'd like to talk to the cleaning woman who found Ruby."

Golick raised his eyebrows. "Inez isn't here. Although she's only been working here for three weeks, she asked for this weekend off. Something about some business she has to take care of."

"Perhaps you can tell me where Inez lives," Mama suggested.

Jeff took a deep breath, clearly aggravated by an interview he felt was going on too long. "Two miles past the interstate, turn left, cross the railroad, first dirt road on the right, third house on the right. Her last name is Moore."

"Thank you, Mr. Golick," Mama said, standing. She thought for a minute. "Did Ruby happen to make any phone calls while she was here?"

"I've given that list to the sheriff."

"It would be helpful if you could check the number of times she stayed at the motel in the past six months, as well as any phone numbers she might have called during that same period," Mama told him.

Jeff let out an exasperated sigh. "I don't see any reason for that."

Mama looked confidently into his eyes, her smile gentle. "I was just thinking that if Abe called you and asked for such a list, it would be nice if you would have already had it made up."

Jeff shrugged, his eyes angry, his face impatient. We thanked him and left the office.

"We're off to find Inez's house?" I asked.

"Exactly," Mama said.

Inez Moore's house was three miles away from the Avondale Inn on a dirt road that runs every bit of a mile from the paved turnoff. It was a road filled with so many potholes that the drive felt like a roller-coaster ride. We ended up in the yard of a tiny un-painted house that had a porch that ran its length. From the outside, it appeared that there were no more than three rooms to the shack. The roof was rusty tin, the yard was dirt. There wasn't even a patch of grass.

All around the yard were six or seven dilapidated cars surrounded by mounds of car tires. Behind the house were trees and what looked like more old, rusty cars. The smell of burning rubber was a stench in the air.

"This must be where everybody in the county abandons their automobiles," I told Mama, looking around and wrinkling up my nose.

"It looks pretty bad, doesn't it?" Mama agreed.

"If Sarah Jenkins knew about this place, she'd stir up the County Council to put an end to the burning of those tires."

"She'd probably tell them that the fumes aggravated her chest condition so much she felt like she wasn't going to take her next breath."

"Burning tires can cause respiratory problems. Come to think of it, isn't there a county ordinance against burning?" I asked.

Mama nodded. "It's against Otis County's ordinances. But nothing in Otis gets enforced unless somebody complains."

Just then a young woman of about twenty-five walked out onto the front porch.

"Jeff phoned and told me to be on the lookout

for you," she called, her voice cold and hard. "I don't know what I can tell you, but since you've gone out of your way to find me, come on up and take a seat."

Mama glanced at me, and headed for Inez Moore's front porch.

By the time we'd climbed the rickety wooden steps, Inez had gone back inside and brought out another chair. "I always thought that fool Ruby would go and kill herself. She was just that crazy!"

"You knew Ruby well?" Mama asked.

Inez was a short woman, less than five feet. She had large hips and legs but a small waist and bosom. Her face was shrewd, her eyes close to each other. At Mama's question, she nodded. "Ruby and I worked at the sewing room in Bartow together." She hesitated. "Three weeks ago I heard there was an opening at the Avondale Inn, so I was the first to ask Jeff for the job. He gave it to me and I said good-bye to sewing piece goods at that factory."

"I see," Mama said.

"Ruby had no need to look for another job. She coulda stayed there at the factory as long as she wanted because she was in the boss's pocket."

Mama's brow crinkled. "You're saying that Ruby's job was secure because she was a good worker?"

"She worked but I know for a fact that her work wasn't what kept her job secure!"

"So what did?"

Inez shrugged. "What does it matter? She went and killed herself and I'm stuck making beds."

"What do they sew at that factory?" Mama asked.

"Sweaters, scarves, gloves. Things northerners need in the dead of winter."

Mama looked interested. "Ruby probably had a lot of scarves?"

"We were allowed two scarves apiece from each lot," Inez replied. "Ruby Spikes followed the rules—two scarves were all she'd take."

"Jeff Golick tells me that Ruby had on a scarf when she checked into the motel on Friday night."

"Don't know about that. First time I had a look at Ruby since I left the plant was when I walked into that room and there she was, dead. She had on a nightgown. I didn't see a scarf."

"Tell me, how did you happen to find Ruby's body?"

"I've already talked to Abe about that."

"I know," Mama said. "But I'd really like to hear the story myself."

Inez threw Mama a strange look. "Why are you so interested in Ruby Spikes?"

"It may be that Ruby didn't kill herself," Mama explained patiently. "Somebody could have slipped into Ruby's room and killed her."

Inez's shrewd eyes grew wide. "Is that what Abe told you?" she demanded.

"It's a thought," Mama admitted.

"Listen, I didn't even know that Ruby Spikes was in the Inn that night. I went to clean her room the next morning like I was supposed to do," she answered, her eyes cautious, like she was concentrating on the details of how she found Ruby's body. "This is the way I work: I go along my floor and knock on each door. 'Cleaning woman here,' I say loud enough for anyone inside to hear me. Most people say something to let me know that they've heard me. Then when I start working each room, they're already getting out of my way. So when I got to the room that Ruby was staying in—Room 217—I knocked and called like I always do. The door slid open 'cause it wasn't locked. That surprised me. I knocked again and said, 'Cleaning woman is here!' The door opened wider. That's when I saw Ruby's legs sprawled out on the floor. I ran right down to the office and got Jeff. When we went back to Room 217, we saw Ruby." Inez paused.

"The sheriff came," Mama prodded gently. "After he and his deputy finished their investigation, who cleaned Room 217?"

"I did," Inez answered hotly, "but that wasn't until over a week later and I ain't took nothing out of it. Besides, up until that time, I wasn't allowed in that room. No one was. Not even Jeff."

"When you finally cleaned the room, did you see anything?" Mama asked. "You know, something of Ruby's the sheriff might have left behind?"

"Like what?" Inez asked it defiantly.

"I suspect the sheriff took all of Ruby's personals," I suggested.

"Maybe," Mama murmured. "I just wanted to make sure nothing was left accidentally in that room."

"There wasn't anything of Ruby's left in that room and like I've already told you, I didn't take anything out of it!" Inez said angrily.

Mama folded her hands in her lap. Then she asked, "Did you know Ruby's boyfriend? The man she used to meet at the Inn?"

Inez frowned. "You think *he* killed Ruby?"

Mama didn't answer.

Inez cocked her head at an angle. "Come to think of it, I saw him in Avondale sometime after midnight that night. My old man and I was coming in from taking care of some business. I blew the horn at him and he waved back at us."

"Sooner or later, Abe is going to have to talk to him," Mama told Inez. She took out her notebook and wrote her telephone number on it, then held the page out to Inez. "If you run into Ruby's friend, tell him if he would talk to me, I'd appreciate it—tell him that our conversation could be considered a private matter."

Inez took the slip from Mama's hand.

"One more question, Inez. Did anybody at the Inn mention to you that they heard the shot that killed Ruby?"

Inez shook her head. "There were only two rooms occupied that night—a trucker who sleeps so hard he wouldn't hear the Lord coming to get him. Then there was the older couple, but their room was clear on the other end of the motel. They told Abe they didn't hear anything."

"Is Charles Parker Ruby's boyfriend?" Mama asked point-blank.

Inez Moore looked puzzled. She shook her head. "I don't know a Charles Parker," she told Mama.

So why did I think she was lying?

CHAPTER
SEVEN

$\mathbf{W}$e were sitting in my car. It struck me as odd that the people immediately on the scene after Ruby's demise couldn't find any sympathy for the woman. Jeff Golick was clearly indifferent; Inez Moore was downright hostile. "Inez didn't have a very friendly attitude, did she?" I said, sharing my thoughts with Mama.

My mother shook her head. "Inez is an angry woman, one that's explosive, one that doesn't keep wrathful feelings hid inside."

"If, in her depression, Ruby's journey to the motel was a cry for help, she came to the wrong place. Saying that, I can't help but wonder why did Ruby come to the motel to die? Why didn't she just kill herself in her own house?"

Mama thought for a moment although I didn't get the impression that the question caught her off guard. Knowing her as well as I do, it was something she'd already considered. "The talk around town is that Herman Spikes was in the Otis Motel that night with that silly girl Betty Jo Mets so Ruby would have been home alone."

I was surprised. Mama doesn't usually speak uncomplimentarily about a person. "Why do you call Betty Jo silly?" I prodded.

"I'm Betty Jo's case manager. I know for a fact that she's a lousy mother and she sleeps with anybody that offers her the least bit of money." Mama shook her head slowly. "What I can't figure out is why Herman would prefer Betty Jo to his wife, Ruby."

Abe seemed to have been waiting for us. His smoke-filled office made me think he'd tried to get as much nicotine in his lungs as possible before Mama and I arrived.

Once we were seated, Mama said to him, "Abe, isn't it strange that nobody heard the shot that killed Ruby Spikes?"

Abe shrugged, picked up a book of matches, then threw them back down on his desk. "There were three other people in the motel that night. I talked to them all and not one of them remembered hearing the shot."

"The more I look into Ruby's death, the more questions come up," Mama told her old friend with conviction strong in her voice.

Abe slid Mama a copy of the police report for her to examine. Mama studied the paper for a moment in silence, then handed it to me.

6:00 P.M.	Herman Spikes arrived home.
7:05 P.M.	Ruby Spikes packed a bag and left house.
9:25 P.M.	Herman Spikes picked up Betty Jo Mets and went to the Otis Motel.
6:09 A.M.	Herman Spikes and Betty Jo left the Otis Motel.
9:00 A.M.	Inez Wright finds Ruby Spikes's body.
9:10 A.M.	Jeff Golick calls Otis police.

"I got a statement from Herman," Abe told Mama. "I had Rick talk to Betty Jo. She swears she and Herman were together from nine-thirty until six o'clock Saturday morning."

"Who was on duty at the check-in desk at the Otis Motel when Herman and Betty Jo arrived?" Mama asked.

"Nobody," Abe told her. "Seems that Herman came in about five o'clock Friday evening right after he knocked off from work. That's when he reserved the room."

Mama's eyes widened. "Why in heaven's name did he reserve the room so early?"

Abe rubbed the bridge of his nose. "According to Herman, he liked getting things ready ahead of time."

Mama cleared her throat. Then she said, "Abe, do you have the list of the phone numbers that Ruby called the night of her death?"

"Yeah," Abe replied, digging through a stack of papers on his desk. "She only made two calls. One was to her own house, the other to a Bartow number." Bartow is twenty-five miles from Otis.

"Would you get the phone company to trace the other number for me? It probably belongs to Ruby's boyfriend."

Abe agreed.

"I'm pretty sure that Ruby's boyfriend is *not* the mysterious Charles Parker," Mama told Abe. "I've talked with Inez Moore, the cleaning woman at the Inn who found Ruby's body. She knows Ruby's lover, even though she won't say his name, but she doesn't know a Charles Parker."

Abe's face darkened. "I suppose Inez didn't tell you about the fight she had with Ruby a few weeks ago, did she? For over six months, inventory at the factory kept coming up short and Clyde Thinner, the manager, was getting real concerned. But none of Clyde's efforts to catch the thief paid off. Then one afternoon he got Ruby to pretend she had a bad headache. He had her sit in the back of her car in the plant parking lot.

"According to Ruby, she heard a car come up in the parking lot. She watched as Inez's boyfriend parked directly in front of the door. After a few minutes, she saw Inez come out of the factory and slip a big bundle into the car's trunk. It was during the busiest time of day, late afternoon, when most workers were preoccupied with reaching their daily quotas. Ruby went right inside the plant and reported what she'd seen to Clyde. Clyde called me and I went to Inez's old man's house and found bundles of scarves and gloves. It seems as if Inez stole the stuff and her old man took it up north to one of his cousins who sold them and split the profit with Inez and her old man. Naturally, Inez was fired."

"That explains the hostile attitude I sensed Inez had when we were talking to her about Ruby," Mama told him.

"Clyde told me that two days after Inez was fired, she sat in her car in the plant's parking lot and waited for Ruby to knock off from work. The fire in her eyes was like a dragon, he was told. It was like Inez had lost her mind. People saw her tear into Ruby like she was a piece of meat. It took four or five of Clyde's strongest men to get Inez off Ruby—he claims that several people swear that Inez would have killed Ruby right then and there that very day if she hadn't been stopped."

"That's interesting," Mama said softly.

"The plant headquarters in New York have instructed their lawyers to press charges against Inez, her boyfriend, and his cousin. Seems to me that Inez Moore and her crew are facing serving some time."

"Did Inez know about that?" Mama asked.

"Clyde got the news the day before Ruby died. He told Ruby and he told everybody at the factory. I reckon it wouldn't have been too much of a problem for Inez and her old man to find out that their troubles were just about to begin that same day."

"So it's possible that Inez and her boyfriend could have murdered Ruby," I suggested. "It would have been easy for her to have learned that Ruby was in the Inn, to get a key to her room and give it to her boyfriend. She of all people would know that the motel was almost empty that night. She could stand watch as her old man slipped inside and killed Ruby, then just pretend to find her body the next morning when she went in to clean the room."

"It'll be interesting to know what Inez and her boyfriend were doing the night Ruby died," Abe said.

"She told me and Mama that she was riding in Avondale around midnight," I said.

"She also told us that she saw Ruby's boyfriend in Avondale about the same time," Mama said thoughtfully.

"I'll get Rick to talk to Inez and her old man," Abe said.

"By the way," Mama said to the sheriff, "Jeff Golick told us that Ruby had a scarf around her neck when she checked into the Inn."

"Her clothes were there but a scarf wasn't in that room," he answered.

"I also told Jeff Golick that you would be wanting a list of the dates Ruby spent at the Avondale Inn during the past six months, and the phone numbers she called while she was staying there."

"You want me to call him and remind him to get it for me, right?" he asked Mama.

Mama flashed him a "yes" smile. "Jeff also told me that Ruby had a large sum of money in her purse that night."

"I suspect you'll want to see this too." Abe handed Mama another piece of paper. "Delcena Walker, the teller at the Otis bank, gave this to me. You'll see the savings activity shows that six months ago, in March, Ruby had a balance of $35,000. She'd been withdrawing an average of five hundred dollars a month until finally she withdrew $33,500 in May, almost exactly three months before the date of her death. Her checking account shows that she deposited seven thousand dollars six weeks ago, in July. She withdrew all seven thousand dollars the day before she died."

"There was no money in her motel room?" Mama asked.

"Not a dime," Abe answered.

"Except for the receipt for that five-thousand-dollar certified check you found in Ruby's purse, there's no trace of all that money," Mama murmured.

Abe's expressive face turned sour. "Ruby could have shot herself because the money got away from her," he pointed out.

Mama looked thoughtful. "Did you ask Herman Spikes about Ruby having that much money?"

"Herman told me they kept their money separate."

Mama shook her head. "This is all so puzzling."

"You might as well know that the gun Ruby used to shoot herself was reported stolen by a Jason Tuten who lives near Cypress Creek, not far from your cousin Agatha."

"When?"

"July twentieth. Two days after the attempted rape on Ruby," Abe said.

"When did Jason Tuten say he missed his pistol?"

"He said he usually kept it in his pickup. He was fishing, saw a snake, went to his pickup to get his .22 and it was gone. He came right to the office and reported it stolen."

"Did he know Ruby? Or remember seeing her anytime before he missed his gun?"

"Nope. Jason swore to me that he never met Ruby Spikes, never even heard of her until I mentioned her name."

Mama had a look on her face like she was trying to figure things out. She took a deep breath, then stood up. "This is all so confusing, Abe. Simone, let's go. I want to stop by to check on Sarah before we go back to the house."

My heart sank. "Do we have to visit Sarah tonight?" I asked, not wanting to hear Sarah whine about not having enough money to pay her taxes or the evilness of her neighbor who was lurking about, waiting for her to lose her property.

"Jeff Golick made it clear to us that he got the impression that Ruby didn't have any friends, at least none close enough for her to confide in. But Sarah was Ruby's godmother—Ruby might not have told Sarah everything, but I'm willing to bet there isn't much that Sarah Jenkins, Carrie Smalls, and Annie Mae Gregory don't know about Ruby Spikes."

CHAPTER

EIGHT

There is still a lot of daylight at seven on an August evening. As I opened my car door, I saw a white Volvo 940 parked directly across from Abe's office. The windows on the automobile were darkly tinted, so I couldn't see the driver. Still, I had the distinct feeling that my mother and I were being watched. I started to say something to Mama, then decided it wasn't anything to call attention to; the feeling was so faint it was probably foolish to mention it.

As I had expected, Sarah Jenkins's comrades, Carrie Smalls and Annie Mae Gregory, were keeping vigil with her on her front porch. "Candi," Sarah asked excitedly as Mama walked up the front steps, "have you found who killed poor Ruby?"

It's only because I know my mother well that I saw the shadow of caution cross her face. "Sarah," she replied gently, "how are you feeling this evening?"

"You haven't found anything, have you?" Sarah asked without answering Mama's question.

Mama shook her head. "No."

"Simone, go in the house and fetch you and your mama a chair," Carrie Smalls ordered, shaking her head as if she was not pleased with Sarah jumping right on Mama about Ruby before offering her a chair to sit in. "Might as well sit down and rest your feet."

I hurried inside, found two folding chairs in the kitchen, and brought them out to the porch.

"Sarah," Mama said once she was seated, "I've talked to a few people and—"

Sarah cut in. *"Ruby didn't kill herself, Candi.* I tell you, that girl didn't shoot herself and you've got to prove it by August thirtieth. I've never been so embarrassed in all my life. Everybody is talking about me, saying that I was stupid to send my tax money to Canada—you'd think the people in Otis are the smartest people in the world! The only way I can stop their wagging tongues is to pay my taxes on time just like everybody else. And people been calling me trying to steal my land for nothing. It's getting so I can't answer my telephone. I told Carrie and Annie Mae that is the only way I can shut the mouths of the people in this town and stop them from talking about me and my business like I was some low-life—"

Mama interrupted. "Tell me something about Ruby. Who were her people? Where did she come from?"

Sarah took a breath. "Ruby was born in the country outside of Bartow. Her mother married one of my cousins. Cousin Sam was from my mother's side, the poor folks in my family. He wasn't much. Come to think of it now, during them times there wasn't much to choose from."

"What was Ruby's mother's name?" Mama asked without showing any reaction to Sarah's derogatory remarks about her own family.

"Nina," Sarah whined as if she felt that Mama was asking questions that didn't have anything to do with Ruby's death. "Nina and Sam had two children. Their older child died when he was ten. Had the whooping cough. Ruby was eight at the time. When she was sixteen, her mother died. The next year, Sam accidentally shot himself to death during a hunting trip. Ruby had quit school, was working in the sewing factory."

"You know what I heard this morning, Candi?" Annie Mae asked, as if she, too, was tired of hearing Sarah's whining.

"I declare, I couldn't believe my ears," Carrie added before Sarah could say anything.

"That crazy Betty Jo Mets has moved right into Ruby's house," Annie Mae announced. "Betty Jo is sleeping in Ruby's bed, wearing Ruby's clothes. The girl ain't hardly dead yet and Betty Jo is making herself at home with Ruby's husband."

"I have to admit, it's hard to believe," Mama murmured. But her attention seemed to be elsewhere.

"And Ruby had some nice things. She might have had her faults, but Ruby Spikes knew how to buy the best. It's a pity that tramp will be using them now that she's gone."

Mama looked up as if she had recollected herself and was once again interested in what the women had to say. "Do any of you know whether or not Ruby had a man friend that she had a habit of meeting at the Avondale Inn?"

"Sure, we know that Ruby met a man from Bartow at that place in Avondale." Sarah jumped back into the conversation with full force. "I could have told you that long ago. Both Herman and Ruby slept around. Ruby's sugar daddy was named Leman Moody. He is a tall, good-looking fella who gambles as hard as he works. Now that I think of it, Leman could have killed Ruby. I know for a fact that he'd told Ruby that he was tired of her, that he didn't want anything more to do with her. My pastor's daughter told me that she saw Leman hitting on two other women a few days before Ruby died."

"Things were really going bad for Ruby," I said, thinking about the attempted rape in her own bed, her feud with Inez Moore, her being dumped by her boyfriend, and her husband sleeping with the town's slut.

"Ruby had sense enough to work hard, but that's about all," Sarah replied. "Come to think of it, that girl she worked with, the one that jumped on her and beat her behind in the plant's parking lot, she could have gone to the motel and killed Ruby!"

"You know about the fight between Inez and Ruby?" Mama asked.

"I should have told you about it sooner," Sarah said. "Candi, I've been so upset about my tax money and the vultures that's trying to take my property away from me that I ain't been thinking right. I know there are things I should have told you before now but, well, you understand that I've had so much on my mind."

"I understand," Mama said quietly.

"Fact is, Candi, if I was a betting woman, I'd put my money on that Inez putting a gun to Ruby and trying to fix it so that it looked like Ruby killed herself."

I couldn't help thinking that Sarah's betting instinct hadn't kept her from being swindled of her tax money. But I kept still.

"Did Ruby have a relative named Charles Parker?" Mama asked.

Sarah coughed feebly, like something was tickling her throat. "The only living relative Ruby had other than me was her mama's sister, Laura. And she moved to Philadelphia years ago, before Ruby's mama married Sam. The last thing I heard about Laura was that she was in an old folks' home. If a Charles Parker was some kin to Ruby, I'd be the one to know it," she whimpered, as if suddenly she felt a great attachment to the dead woman.

Mama nodded. "I'm surprised that Ruby didn't

come to you when she was having so many problems."

"Ruby kept to herself like she didn't want me to know her business. The truth is, I don't reckon she came to see me more than two or three times since Nina died, but that didn't stop me from hearing about what she was up to."

"How did it come about that you became Ruby's godmother?" Mama asked Sarah.

Sarah lifted her chin. "It was one of those things that just happened without warning. The Sunday morning Nina planned to have the baby christened, she came to my house in tears. The woman who had offered to be the child's godmother decided not to do it. It was too late for Nina to find somebody else. She asked me to stand with her to be the child's godmother, saying that she wouldn't expect anything more from me. After both Nina and Sam died, I took out this little policy on the girl, figuring that if something happened to her, I'd end up having to be the one most likely to see to burying her. Fact is, Ruby got married and even though my obligation ended, I still kept the policy. Didn't think much of it until after Ruby's body was found."

"So you didn't know about the man who slipped in through Ruby's back window and tried to rape her?"

"She didn't tell me about that either," Sarah said. "Like I said, Ruby kept to herself. But I heard talk about what happened. A woman on the other side of town told me she overheard Ruby talking on the phone at the plant. Whoever she was speaking to,

Ruby told that person that if it wasn't for the fact that Herman came driving up during the time she was wrestling with her attacker, she didn't think she could have held out much longer."

Mama asked, "Sarah, do you have an address for Ruby's aunt Laura?"

Sarah thought for a moment. "If I do, I can't remember where I put it."

"It's the right thing to do to notify her that Ruby's dead, don't you think?" Mama asked gently.

Annie Mae crossed her arms under her large bosom. "Candi, I've got a cousin in Philadelphia who keeps up with folks who move there from Otis. If you want me to, I'll call her and ask her to look up Ruby's aunt—let her know that her only niece done gone to her reward."

"I'd like the phone number and the address of Ruby's aunt myself," Mama said as if it were an afterthought. "I'd like to be the one to tell Laura about Ruby's demise."

"Suit yourself," Annie Mae said. "As soon as I can get an address and a telephone number, I'll give it to you."

Mama stood.

"Candi, if I remember anything else that will help you track down who went into the motel room in Avondale and killed Ruby, I'll call you," Sarah said. But I couldn't tell if the tears in her eyes were for herself or for the dead woman.

"I know you will," Mama responded kindly before she eased off the front porch and headed for my car.

CHAPTER
NINE

We got home at a quarter to nine. I went to the backyard, where my father was playing with Midnight, and said hello, then I went into the kitchen, poured two glasses of iced tea for me and Mama, and waited for her to join me.

Mama, on the other hand, wasn't interested in something cold to drink on a hot August evening. Instead, she went straight to the phone and called Abe. She asked whether or not he knew Leman Moody.

Abe told Mama that Leman Moody and a man nicknamed Fingers had gotten into a fight three months earlier over a gambling debt. Both had spent a day in the Otis County jail. Mama thanked Abe for the information and hung up.

No sooner had Mama joined me at the table and picked up her glass of tea than the phone rang. I glanced at the kitchen clock. Nine o'clock. Mama picked up the phone, and less than three minutes later her conversation was over.

"That was Leman Moody," she told me. "He wants us to meet him in the parking lot of the Avondale Inn."

"Now?"

Mama nodded, then walked out back to tell my father of our plans. I'd just taken my first sip of iced tea when she was back in the kitchen, picking up her purse, and motioning me toward the door.

In the brightness of sunlight, the drive from Otis to Avondale is beautiful. Pine trees line both sides of the highway. At nine-fifteen on a night when the moon is new, however, the darkness drapes the fifteen-mile stretch in a blackness that's only occasionally pierced by the glowing eyes of raccoons, possums, or deer. The highway is virtually empty at night, seldom used by the locals since the advent of the interstate. As I drove, I felt a growing apprehension. "What does this Leman Moody want with us at this hour of the night?" I asked Mama.

"I sent him the message that I wanted to talk to him, remember? I'm sure Inez Moore got in touch with him as soon as we left her house."

"Why couldn't he come to Otis?"

"I didn't ask," Mama said, her tone short the way it gets when she doesn't want to do a lot of talking.

"Suppose this Leman Moody killed Ruby. Suppose he'll try to kill us."

"Simone, you're exaggerating again," Mama murmured.

"Okay, I'm putting it on, but I don't like this. Something tells me we shouldn't be going to Avondale tonight."

"Tell that something that we have to find out whether Ruby committed suicide or not."

"Mama, that's not funny. You're always talking about instincts—your instinct tells you this or that. Well, right now my instinct tells me that we shouldn't be going to Avondale tonight!"

Mama's head turned toward me, and although I couldn't see the expression on her face, I sensed my concern had gotten her attention.

"We'll be careful," she reassured me.

As we pulled up in the Avondale Inn's parking lot, a sleek black Mercedes pulled out. Six or seven cars in the lot made me think that there were more people staying in the Inn than the night Ruby died.

We sat quietly, looking out the car window. "What now?" I asked my mother after we'd been waiting over five minutes.

"Leman told me he'd be here," Mama replied. "We'll wait a little longer."

It was then that a white Volvo circled, then parked directly in front of us. The lights were switched off, the driver's door opened. A tall, lean man approached us, his face in shadow. I felt my heart start to beat a little faster.

"What this I hear about you putting the word out that somebody killed Ruby instead of her killing herself?" the man asked without greeting us.

"Can we go someplace and talk, Mr. Moody?" Mama suggested. "Maybe across the street at the McDonald's?"

Leman Moody hesitated. "Okay," he finally said, not bothering to hide his reluctance.

McDonald's had few patrons, although the drive-thru seemed busy. We sat in the back of the restaurant. Even though Leman Moody wore dark glasses, I could feel his unblinking stare. "I'm asking again, what this I hear that somebody killed Ruby?" he insisted in his gravelly voice.

If Leman's tone worried Mama, her face didn't show it. "Did you see Ruby the night she died?"

Leman took a deep breath and let it out, then he glanced toward the front of the room. I followed his glance but saw nothing. "No," he answered to the empty space, as if someone were there, listening.

Mama gave him a curious look. "What about Ruby's money?"

Leman's head turned; he faced Mama again. "What little bit of money Ruby loaned me isn't worth talking about. Besides, I planned to pay her back. No matter what had happened between us, I had all intention of paying her every cent, and she knew that!"

"I understand that Ruby had a large sum of money

a few weeks before she died. And that money seems to be missing."

"What Ruby had was her business. What she loaned me was our business, and she didn't loan me no large sum of money and don't you go telling nobody anything differently. I ain't looking for trouble but I ain't scared of causing trouble when it's due. Don't you be going around throwing my name in the pot with Ruby. What went on between us was mutual. Ruby understood where I stood from the first day I took up with her."

"I heard that you broke up with Ruby just before she died. Is that true?"

"So what if I did? Listen, if you want to point a finger at somebody, talk to the people at that factory. I wasn't the only person who didn't want anything else to do with her after she helped set up Inez and her old man. And there is that husband of hers. Talk is that she was about to dump him 'cause he wasn't treating her right. That woman was off her rocker, taking pills to sleep and pills to wake up. Maybe she forgot what pills she'd taken and overdosed herself."

"But Ruby didn't overdose on medication," Mama reminded him. "She was shot."

"I don't know anything about that!"

Once again, very quietly, Mama asked Leman, "Are you sure that you didn't see Ruby the night she died?"

"I don't know what makes you think that I've got

to tell you anything." Leman hesitated. "But the last time I saw Ruby was when she knocked off work at four o'clock that day. We had a big shipment to get out, so I worked another four hours. When I got home that night I was bone-tired. Soon as I took my bath I went straight to my bed."

Mama leaned forward. "I was told that you were in Avondale around midnight the night Ruby died."

"Who told you that?" Leman asked. There was a trace of uneasiness in his eyes.

"Somebody saw you," Mama told him, her voice low, calm.

"That somebody lied to you. Like I told you, I'd worked twelve hours straight that night. I came home, took a bath, and crashed."

"Do you know Charles Parker?" Mama asked.

"No," he answered.

Mama tilted her head a little.

Leman stood up to leave, took a breath as if to say something, then didn't. He left us, pushing through the restaurant's door and into the warm darkness.

Something's wrong, I thought. I glanced at the speedometer. Sixty miles an hour, a cruising speed on the dark and desolate road from Avondale to Otis. So why is my heart pounding?

Then the hood of my Honda flew up in my face.

I hit the brakes. Mama reached out and grabbed my arm but then quickly released it when she realized how tight my fingers were wrapped around the steering wheel and how hard I was struggling to blindly keep the car on the road.

"Take it easy, Simone!" she shouted as the smell of rubber and asphalt recorded the Honda's disastrous skid.

The darkness confused me and the Honda spun around, left the pavement, flew up in the air and nose-dived in straight down.

Then all was silent, except for the trickle of some fluid running somewhere in the darkness of the car.

My body ached like I'd been used as a punching bag. "Mama," I whispered.

Nothing.

I tried to turn, but my seat belt and the air bag pinned me tight. "Mama, are you all right?" I shouted.

Nothing.

Then, feeling myself a long way off and drifting farther into darkness, I decided that my mother was dead and I hadn't told her good-bye.

CHAPTER
TEN

The trip to Otis County General Hospital's emergency room in the ambulance was a nightmare that I was glad to have over. We were lucky: a man driving by had spotted our wreck and called 911 to say that a car had gone off into a ditch.

"Nothing broken. Nothing fractured, not even a concussion," the doctor told us, his voice devoid of emotion. "You can go home."

My father smiled nervously. "Thank God," he told Mama. "I don't know what I would have done if I'd lost both you and Simone at the same time."

It was almost one A.M. when we finally got home. Other than reassuring my father that we would be just fine, Mama hadn't said very much. When my father asked, "What happened out there?" she simply told him, "Maybe tomorrow it'll all make sense."

Mama's words told me that she, like me, was trying to understand what had really happened to us. The hood of the Honda—why would it go up like that? Had somebody snapped the latch? If so, they'd have to undo the lock from the inside of the car. I tried to remember: Did I lock the car door when we went into McDonald's? And who was the Good Samaritan who had called Abe?

It was almost noon before I opened my eyes. My body hurt all over, so the first thing I did was to take a steaming hot shower. I almost felt human by the time I stumbled into the kitchen.

Mama sat at the table, sipping coffee.

"What's up, pretty lady?" I asked.

"You all right?" she responded without looking at me.

"Except for soreness, I'm terrific. What about you?"

"I'm okay," she said, her voice distracted, her mind somewhere else. "Your breakfast is in the microwave."

"Thanks. Where's Daddy?"

"James has gone to get the car towed. I suspect you'll need a rental to get back to Atlanta."

"Today is Sunday, isn't it? I wonder whether my car can be fixed."

"James will take care of that," Mama said.

I poured my coffee and orange juice. "Have you decided what happened out there?" I asked, taking a plate of golden waffles from the microwave and joining her at the table.

"Simone," Mama said, "why would that hood fly up like that?"

I looked into her eyes; the concern was deep. I picked up my fork, then put it back down. For once, even Mama's wonderful food wasn't tempting. We'd almost died on the road from Avondale to Otis. *Why?*

"Could it have been Leman Moody?" Mama continued. "And, if so, why? I didn't say anything that would have threatened him, did I?"

"Of course not," I said, but I didn't sound as soothing as I'd hoped. "It could just as well have been Inez Moore or her old man."

Mama nodded but didn't say anything. It was as if she was following some thought inside her head.

"Up until you started asking questions," I said, "the consensus has been that Ruby Spikes committed suicide. The killer might have been satisfied that was going to be the end of it."

"Yes," Mama said. "But this only confirms that somebody killed Ruby, doesn't it? If what happened to us was no accident, Ruby's death wasn't a suicide."

I nodded. "You'd better be careful," I warned. "The killer may try again!"

"Yes," she murmured, "but I'd rather James not know what we suspect just now. He'd panic and do something to scare the killer."

"That lunatic should be scared! Mama, we almost

died last night. And it's really true: my whole life flashed in front of my eyes when I thought I was going to die!"

"Simone, honey, you're exaggerating again."

"Okay, but it was a close call and you know it. When I called you and you didn't answer, I just knew you were dead. And, lady, that's pretty scary!"

"I was stunned," she admitted softly. "Confused, I guess. I heard your voice but—"

I reached over and squeezed her hands. "No need to apologize," I said. "We got through that alive, that's what counts."

The front door opened and closed.

"Candi," my father said as he walked into the kitchen. "There is a skid mark where you and Simone had your accident last night that looks like somebody pushed the Honda in the ditch."

"Really?" Mama said, trying to look surprised.

"And the back fender on the car is dented, like it might have been the spot that took the blow," he added, shaking his head.

"Things happened fast," Mama said. "Do you want a cup of coffee?"

"No," Daddy answered. "You know, baby, both Abe and I think there's more to what happened than a freak accident. Do either you or Simone remember being hit from the rear?"

"Maybe the person who called Abe to report our car in the ditch bumped us accidentally?" I suggested. "Maybe, because of the darkness, he saw us too late and—"

"If it happened that way, I guess whoever called Abe did the right thing. Although he should've stayed around to make sure you and your mama were okay."

"If he was alone in the car, he had no other choice but to get to a phone and report the accident. Everybody knows that the chances of another car driving on that road that time of night are nil," I said.

My father seemed to relax. "Abe said that the caller didn't give a name."

"Whoever made that call saved our lives," I told him, hoping this interpretation would satisfy his concern about the skid mark and dented back fender.

"I guess so," my father said reluctantly. But it was clear from his tone that he wasn't sure that my story was really what had happened to me and Mama as we drove back from Avondale the night before.

CHAPTER

ELEVEN

I stayed in Otis until Monday morning, when my father helped me arrange for the Honda's repair and a two-week rental of a Ford Escort. I arrived in Atlanta late Monday afternoon. The balance of the week was hectic, but Friday morning was a demon.

First thing that happened was that I got a ticket. The residential area off Piedmont onto Morningside is always targeted for speeders. I'd seen at least a dozen people get tickets there, but for some reason their sad experience escaped me this morning. I was driving fifty in a twenty-five-mile-an-hour zone when I got nipped right after I came over the small hill that's down from Morningside Elementary School. That meant a $125 fine.

Once I finally got to the office and tried to make a pot of coffee, the darn machine wouldn't turn on. Shirley, Sidney's assistant, called the company that services it. They told her it would be three days before they could get us another machine to replace it. So I had to make coffee the hard way, the way it was done in the Stone Age: put a cup of water in the microwave, boil it, and then use instant coffee. While my water was being nuked in the microwave, I discovered I had a run in my pantyhose an inch and a half wide that ran straight up my right leg. I groaned.

The only thing to do, I was thinking once I'd gotten back in my office with my cup of instant coffee, was to go down the street to buy another pair of stockings. That thought hadn't cleared my mind when my boss walked into my office. "Simone," Sidney snapped in an unusual tone, "this brief has so many typos in it, I refuse to read it!"

"Two of our typists are out with the flu," I reminded him. "And the temp we hired just can't cut it—she's not familiar with legal terms."

Sidney wasn't satisfied. He threw the papers on my desk. "Get this corrected!" he roared, thrusting his face a little too close to mine. I noticed that there were tiny white flakes of dandruff on his shoulders. "I want it back on my desk *today*!" Then he stomped out.

For a moment, I didn't know what to do. Finally, I decided to do the corrections myself. It would be the best way to make sure that they were done right, the way that Sidney always wanted it.

Then my computer went down. I went into the secretaries' office: the whole system had crashed. "Now that we can't live without them," I told Shirley, "the machines have started to exercise their control over us."

"Maybe they're like all the rest of us overworked laborers," Shirley grumbled. "They stop when they've been pushed too far."

Uh-oh, I thought, Sidney must have taken an angry swipe at her this morning, too.

"I'll call the repairman," Shirley told me. "I'll make sure he understands that we need him ASAP."

It wasn't ten minutes later that I was at the copier and *that* sucker jammed. I pulled paper from every nook and cranny I could see, but to no avail. The message light kept flashing "Jammed." Reluctantly, I had to go back to Shirley.

When I told her what had happened, she demanded, "What do you want me to do?"

"Call another repairman," I suggested, bracing myself for another fit of temper.

"I'll call in a minute." Her tone told me that I'd been dismissed from her presence. I shrugged and headed back to my office. I drank two more cups of instant coffee, and cursed the run in my stocking at least a dozen times until I decided to leave the office early and stop by Lenox Mall before lunch. Just as I made that decision, the phone rang. It was Cliff. Cliff has eyes that remind me of Richard Roundtree's, deep, dark, and sensuous. Today, however, his voice didn't sound sexy. It sounded exasperated. "I have to break our lunch date," he told me.

"What's the matter now?" I asked, no doubt sounding more than a little impatient.

"It's Daniel Abrams. That man won't give me a break."

Daniel Abrams was Cliff's client. He was an accountant, a man who got his kicks knowing where every penny of his money was twenty-four hours a day. Daniel Abrams's divorce was now final. Cliff's law firm had given him an itemized bill for the services rendered. Now Abrams wanted proof that x amount of dollars had indeed been spent on postage, telephone calls, copying, etc., and it would take Cliff all afternoon to satisfy this man so that the firm could finally get paid for hours and hours of work.

"Will he keep you through dinner?" I asked.

"Heck no," Cliff said. "And he'll be told that I'm leaving town tomorrow and I won't be back until Monday noon."

"That means we'll have an uninterrupted weekend."

"Sounds good to me," Cliff said enthusiastically and hung up. I decided to walk across the street and get lunch, which turned out to be a tuna-fish sandwich that didn't taste like tuna and a diet Coke that had more ice in it than Coke. Maybe that was the diet part.

Around three o'clock, I called Mama. "How are things going?" I asked.

"Okay."

"Cliff wants to get out of town for the weekend."

"Great. Bring him home. I'll make a meal especially for him. What time can I expect you two?"

"We'll be there by nine o'clock in the morning."

Going to Otis suited me fine. It would give me another opportunity to work on party plans with Mama. Her cooking would be the thing to ease the anxieties Cliff was having over his penny-pinching client. And I'd get to hear firsthand what was going on in Mama's private investigation into the murder of Ruby Spikes.

CHAPTER

TWELVE

Cliff's favorite dish is Mama's skillet-roasted lemon chicken with potatoes.

Mama was just sliding this dish from the oven as Cliff and I walked into her kitchen. She'd also fixed fresh string beans, glazed carrots, sliced tomatoes, a tossed salad, and a sweet-potato pie that threatens waistlines. We all sat right down to eat.

"Candi, I've done what you asked," Daddy said thirty minutes later as he dished himself a second helping of chicken and potatoes. "Neither Coal nor I could come up with the fella who wore a shirt like that piece of material you showed me last week. The more we thought about it, the more we drew a blank."

Mama looked disappointed. "I appreciate your efforts, James," she said as the telephone rang. She excused herself from the table.

"What shirt?" I asked my father.

"Ruby Spikes tore a piece off the shirt of the man who tried to rape her. Candi got it from Abe. She wanted to know whether or not Coal or I had ever seen it on any one of the fellas who hang out at Joe's Pool Hall."

Mama came back into the room. Her face looked like it does when she's trying to figure something out but can't quite seem to put her finger on it. "Betty Jo Mets is dead," she told us in a stunned voice. "She called me just last night, said she was confused about something and needed to talk with me. I suspected she wanted to know something about the care of her boys, because she asked me to meet her at Portia Bolton's house this afternoon."

"Who is Portia Bolton?" I asked.

"Portia is the foster mother I placed Betty Jo's two little boys with. She is a fine woman. She never had any children of her own, but she's the kind of woman whose care children thrive under."

I pushed back my chair. Mama motioned me to sit back down. "Finish eating," she said to me. "I told Abe we'd be at his office in a half an hour."

"Did Betty Jo have some kind of an ailment that could account for her dying so suddenly?" my father asked.

"If she did, I didn't know about it," Mama said.

"What happened to her?" I asked, not liking the look on Mama's face.

She shook her head sadly. "Abe told me that the

paramedics called him. They'd gotten a call from Herman two hours ago. Herman told them that Betty Jo hadn't responded to his efforts to wake her—I can't believe she's dead, she sounded so alive last night when I spoke with her!"

We arrived at Abe's office around two o'clock.

"Tell me exactly what happened," Mama said as soon as we entered.

Abe didn't hesitate. "This is Herman's story," he said, toying with an unlit cigarette. "He and Betty Jo went to bed around nine last night. Betty Jo slept through the night as usual—Herman swears he heard her breathing. Anyway, when he got up this morning, Betty Jo was still asleep. He left the house and returned around ten A.M. He did some chores in the backyard before he went into the house. He was surprised to find that Betty Jo hadn't gotten out of bed. He tried to wake her. That's when he realized that she'd stopped breathing. He called 911. The paramedics came. They told him that Betty Jo was dead and that she'd been dead for hours, so instead of taking her to the hospital they called the medical examiner."

"When did you arrive at Herman's house?" Mama asked Abe.

"I got there before the body was moved to the morgue. Betty Jo was in the bed, looking like she was in a deep sleep. There was an empty glass on the side of her bed. I had it sent to the lab but it looks to me that she died in her sleep. Maybe a blood vessel burst in her head."

"An aneurysm," I volunteered.

"I suppose you've ordered an autopsy?" Mama asked him.

Abe nodded. "I sure have. I called Charleston Medical Center yesterday. It will be a while before I get Ruby's autopsy report because the work is backed up but the doctor is back on the job."

"Betty Jo called me last night," Mama told Abe. "She asked me to meet her today at Portia Bolton's house."

Abe's eyebrow rose.

"Nothing Betty Jo said to me gave me the impression that she'd be dead today," Mama told him.

"Time and life catch up with everybody," Abe reminded her.

"Yes," Mama answered softly. "I'm just surprised that they caught up with Betty Jo so soon."

From the look on Portia Bolton's face, it was clear that she already knew that Betty Jo was dead. "News travels fast," she said, greeting us on her porch and motioning us inside. "The noonday news reported that Herman had found her body."

The living room we now stood in held an easy chair and a couch, both covered tidily with pale blue sheets. A small table stood next to the couch, pictures of two boys neatly arranged on it. Newly hung white curtains were at the windows. The smell of Clorox was heavy in the air.

Portia offered us a seat. "The way Betty Jo lived, nothing would surprise me about her. Still, I didn't think she'd die so young!"

"Did she call you last night?" Mama asked.

"No," Portia replied, looking concerned. "Was she suppose to have called me?"

"Last night she called and asked me to meet her here today," Mama said. "I thought she might have called you and told you she'd be coming."

"No," Portia said, shaking her head.

"When was the last time she visited her boys?"

"The day before yesterday. Herman brought her here and then drove off. An hour later he picked her up again. Lord knows how I'm going to tell those boys that she won't be coming to see them again, especially since she told them that she was going to bring them their big old tomcat from her place," Portia said sadly.

Mama leaned over and patted her hand. "I'll arrange for a psychologist to talk with them," she said.

Portia nodded, grateful. "Mack is eight and little Curtis is only six. It was hard enough for me to help them understand why they couldn't live with their own mama. Now to explain to them that one day she was alive and happy and the next day she's dead . . . Candi, I don't know how those two sweet boys are going to take it!"

"We'll help them understand," Mama promised.

"We'll do whatever it takes to help them through this. Let me ask you something, Portia. Did you have a chance to talk to Betty Jo when she visited two days ago?"

Portia nodded. "Like I told you, Betty Jo was happy, grinning from ear to ear. She liked living with Herman. She boasted that she wore Ruby's clothes, strutted her rings and watches. Betty Jo couldn't talk enough about the good time she was having."

Mama sat up straight.

"Betty Jo even gave each of her boys a twenty-dollar bill—those bills looked like they'd just come off the printing press," Portia continued. "Fact is, I almost had a stroke when Betty Jo opened up her pocketbook and pulled that brand new money out. Look like the Treasury had just printed it. As soon as she left, I had to take Curtis and Mack to the new Wesmart to buy a toy. That money nearly burned a hole in their pockets." She smiled. "I couldn't bear to spend such clean, pretty money, so I gave them two old twenties that I had been saving for a living room set. I put their new bills up for safekeeping. In six months, when I've saved enough money for a set, I'll have to use it. Right now, though, having new money will bring good fortune to my house."

"It's a tragedy that Betty Jo died so young," Mama commented. "She couldn't be more than twenty-five."

"Fact is," Portia said, "I don't remember hearing that she had a condition that might have caused her sudden death. But then, death can come sudden to most anybody, can't it?"

Mama murmured her agreement.

"I wonder . . ." Portia said, her face clouding.

"What?" Mama asked.

"Betty Jo promised the boys that she'd bring their cat, Sparkle, here for them to take care of. It seems that now that she was living with Herman she wasn't able to go back to her own house every day to feed the cat."

"There's no reason that those boys can't have their cat," Mama agreed.

"I'll go pick it up first thing in the morning," Portia said, smiling. "It'll be a comfort to Mack and Curtis."

We rose to leave the house. Outside, two handsome little boys were playing with toy trucks under a tree in the yard. Mama called to them. Curtis and Mack looked up, giggled, and waved, grinning from ear to ear.

"I'll set up an appointment with the county's psychologist," Mama reminded Portia, whose eyes had filled with tears at the sight of the two happy, noisy boys. "Don't you worry about them."

"Candi," Portia said, "does this mean that I'll be able to keep the boys now?" She sounded anxious.

Mama smiled at her. "It's what you want, isn't it?"

"They're good boys, lots of company for me. I love them as if they were my own, and you know I'd do anything for them."

"I'll see what I can do," Mama promised just before we got into the car and pulled away.

Our next stop: Cousin Agatha's house. Daddy's first cousin is a tall, lanky woman with the business mind of the family. The Covington family owns a lot of property; Agatha had it put in a land corporation. She administers the corporation business, sees that all the taxes are paid, and when possible, she gets the timber cut and has the funds distributed throughout the family.

Agatha never married, and as far as I know, never wanted to. She took care of her father, Chester Covington, until his death last year. Now she spends her free time working with the senior citizens at the Community Center.

"It seems like Agatha likes taking care of old people," I said to Mama as we drove to Cypress Creek, where Agatha lived.

"She works with the senior citizens as fervently as she took care of Uncle Chester," Mama answered. "I guess taking care of the elderly is Agatha's calling."

Things had changed quite a bit on the Covington homestead since my great-uncle Chester died last year. Agatha had had a lot of work done on the house. White aluminum siding decked its outside; there was a new tiled roof. Agatha had also had the house insulated, and the walls of each room had new, striking wallpaper. Central air-conditioning, something Uncle Chester wouldn't even consider, now cooled the rooms.

There was new furniture, too. New curtains and new carpet as well. Agatha had used her share of the money she had gotten from the cut timber wisely, as everybody in Otis knew she would.

"What have you got on the stove?" Mama asked Agatha the moment we stepped inside.

"Nothing half as good as what's cooking on your stove, Candi," Agatha replied right away.

"Agatha, you're every bit as good a cook as I am," Mama told her, laughing, "and you know it."

Agatha, who tends to be shy, grinned. "What's your mama up to now, Simone?" she asked me.

I smiled back. "She wants a favor," I answered.

Agatha nodded. "I suspected the like."

Mama took a chair and said, "Agatha, I've got something to tell you. Simone, Will, and Rodney want to have a party for me and James."

"Good," Agatha said. "I like parties."

"We don't want Mama to cook," I said.

Agatha's eyes grew wide. "For heaven sakes, why?"

" 'Cause it's their wedding anniversary. Mama shouldn't be cooking. She should be celebrating," I told her.

"You want *me* to cook?" Agatha asked.

"You and Gertrude," Mama answered.

"My cousin ain't a bad cook," Agatha said about Gertrude, "but she can't hold a candle to me."

We all laughed.

"Of course I'll cook for your party, Candi," Agatha agreed, smiling. "Tell me what you want and—"

"Mama has a menu," I told her.

"Good. When is this shindig?"

"It's Saturday, September fifteenth."

Agatha straightened up. "That's four weeks away."

"Is there a conflict?" I asked.

Agatha shook her head. "Ain't no such thing as a conflict when it comes to cooking for James and Candi's anniversary party."

"Then it's settled," Mama said, pleased. "Now I want to change the subject."

Agatha leaned forward, as if she could tell from Mama's tone that they were about to discuss something of extreme importance.

"Agatha, you've been around Otis all of your life," Mama said. "You know just about every family in Otis and its surrounding counties. Do you know a man named Charles Parker?"

Cousin Agatha thought. Then she shook her head. "No, Candi, I don't recollect a single soul from these parts named Charles Parker."

CHAPTER
THIRTEEN

"Let's go to Betty Jo's place before we go back to the house," Mama said to me. "I was thinking that the boys' cat, Sparkle, probably hasn't been fed in days."

Mama told me that Betty Jo lived on the road between Avondale and Otis, which meant that I had to go back through Otis to get to Betty Jo's house.

The sky was calm and clear. I pulled into the Texaco station on the corner of Oak and First to pump some gas. Mama got out of the car and started toward the station's convenience store at the same time as Inez Moore walked out of it.

"Well, Miss Snoopy Snoop, are you still asking questions about Ruby Spikes?"

"How are you doing?" Mama asked Inez, ignoring her unfriendly greeting.

Inez eyed Mama suspiciously. "You don't care how I'm doing. It's *what* I'm doing that you're so worried about."

"I've heard of the trouble Ruby caused you at the plant, the reason you got fired."

"Ruby Spikes was a meddling, sickly sweet, nasty-nice woman that made me sick. She did a lot of people a favor by shooting herself!"

"I can understand why you'd feel that way," Mama said to her, again not responding to her hostility.

Inez folded her arms across her chest and leaned toward Mama, her eyes blazing with rage, but Mama didn't back away. "Listen, lady, I ain't the only person who Ruby did a favor by leaving this world. Sure, she stopped my little game at the plant, but that boyfriend of hers used her up, getting money from her to pay off his gambling debts. He told me himself that he was tired of her. And her husband, I reckon he's glad that people ain't laughing at him anymore. The whole town called Herman Spikes stupid. He pretended that he didn't care about his wife giving her money and her body to a womanizing gambler like Leman Moody, but everybody knew it cut him to his heart!"

"Herman had his own woman," Mama told her. "He evidently didn't care that Ruby had a thing with Leman."

"Little you know," Inez shot back. "Men can screw around like dogs but they ain't for their wives doing the same thing. Ruby is dead, and that's the end of it. Whatever trouble she caused me, I'll take care of it. I've got a chance to bounce back. Ruby's chances ended the night she killed herself," she said. Then she turned and got into the car that was parked directly in front of my rental car, and sped off.

I paid for the gas, Mama bought us each a bottle of iced tea, and then we got back into the car and headed toward Betty Jo Mets's house.

It turned out that the house was just off the highway on a narrow dirt road, not a hundred yards from the ditch my car had skidded into last week. Surely, I thought as I pulled into the muddy driveway, Betty Jo would have heard the commotion of the accident if she had been at home that night. But she'd been living it up at Ruby's house.

The little place was dilapidated: badly in need of paint, with rows of missing shingles and a definite sag to the roof. All was quiet.

Mama knocked at the front door, although she said she didn't expect an answer. A movement off to the right caught my eye. A large blond and brown cat scurried across the side of the house, then stopped, eyeing us warily. "Mrowr!" he cried, looking ready to jump if we tried to grab him.

"There you are," Mama said softly. "We've come to take you to Curtis and Mack."

The cat sniffed the air.

"Is there something to eat in the car?" Mama asked.

"No," I answered.

"Come on now, Sparkle," Mama again urged. "I want to take you to a nice warm place to sleep, where two little boys will give you more love than you can handle."

"Mrowr!"

"What now?" I asked.

"Go inside. See if you can find something for us to give it to eat."

I peered through the front window, then pushed on the front door. It swung open. I eased inside. The place stank of old garbage and couldn't have consisted of more than four rooms. The one I stood in had two chairs, both dirty and worn. I spotted an empty plate on the floor in the corner of the room.

I hope it's the cat dish, I thought as I picked it up and slipped into the next room to search for something to put in it. I was right in deciding that it was the kitchen. I spotted an unopened can of cat food among the litter of cans and dirty dishes.

I moved fast to open the can, dish up the food, and take it back outside. The cat approached me cautiously. I started to grab him but Mama stopped me. "Give him space, let him eat," she urged.

The cat polished off the food, then sat licking his chops. When Mama reached for him, the cat purred, his body relaxed.

"Get me something to wrap him in," Mama told me, looking at the cat with tenderness.

Once more I went inside the house. I found what looked like a rag and took it out to my mother. She wrapped Sparkle up and handed him to me.

"Put him in the backseat of the car," she told me. "I want to take a look around the place. I won't be long."

The cat looked up at me and purred, his eyes squeezed to mere slits. I felt he was telling me, "Take me, I'm yours."

No sooner had I put him down on the backseat and closed the car door than I heard the first shot. I stood up and looked around, unsure of the direction it had come from. Then I heard the second shot, along with what sounded like a window shattering in the back of the house. "Mama," I screamed, instinctively falling to the ground. I took a deep breath and crawled toward the small house. When I got to the front door, I called to Mama again.

"Simone," her voice came back. "I'm okay."

There was another shot.

I shouted, "I'm coming inside!"

"No," Mama urged. "There's no use in both of us getting killed!"

Mama's words sent an adrenaline rush through my body that felt like a spring flood. I let out a breath and, on my hands and knees, pushed through the front door. There was no way I was going to sit quietly and let my mother be killed.

Mama was in a corner, crouched behind an old chair. My stomach felt like it had been scooped out with a dull plastic spoon on seeing how vulnerable she looked.

"Come over here!" she ordered, no doubt feeling as protective of me as I was of her.

I hesitated. Another shot pushed me toward my mother.

Then all was quiet.

For what seemed like hours, we sat huddled together, our only line of defense an old chair. It was like a great calm after a hurricane.

"What do we do now?" I finally asked Mama.

Before she had a chance to answer, we heard a car door slam. A few minutes later we heard, somewhere in the far distance, the sound of a car engine.

"He's gone," I said, assuming that the shooter was a man and thanking the Lord that he'd decided not to kill us.

"Sounds like it," Mama said, standing and stretching.

"Let's get out of here," I urged, reaching for her hand.

Mama nodded and followed me to the front door. Outside, we looked around. Nothing seemed changed.

We headed for the car and I eased into the driver's seat.

"Simone," Mama said, *"Sparkle is gone!"*

I turned to examine the backseat, where I'd placed the furry animal. He was definitely gone. The only thing remaining were long blond and brown hairs that confirmed I had put him down on that spot.

"You mean somebody tried to kill us for that cat?" I asked.

Mama shrugged, then fell into a reflective silence as I tried to understand why somebody would try to kill us for a cat that had been neglected until we came to rescue it.

When we pulled off the dirt road and onto the paved highway, we spotted a car parked a few feet away. Mama touched my arm.

Leman Moody sat in his white Volvo. Although I couldn't see his eyes through the tinted window, I was sure he was staring at us, watching and waiting.

"He's the one who tried to kill us," I whispered. The words were barely out of my mouth when Leman started his engine and drove off toward the town of Avondale.

❧

When we hit Otis's town limits, Mama made me promise not to tell my father about the shooting or the missing cat.

"I believe that Leman Moody tried to kill us twice," I said. "Aren't you afraid?"

"Simone, I may be afraid of taking a particular step, but I'm not afraid of walking."

"What's that supposed to mean?"

"An incident may be frightening but it doesn't mean that I'll stop seeking the truth."

"I'll bet you anything Leman Moody was the person who pushed us off the road last week—and he tried to finish the job today. Doesn't that scare you?"

"I don't like being shot at or forced into a ditch," Mama told me. "But the fact is, we *weren't* killed. I'm beginning to think somebody's trying to persuade me to stop asking questions about Ruby's death, but that's the path I'm going to continue to walk. Now, Simone, your father is already suspicious about our car accident; he keeps asking me questions. If he finds out what just happened at Betty Jo's place, he'll insist that we stop looking into Ruby's death."

"Daddy might have the right idea," I retorted.

"Simone!" Mama said, her tone saying she wasn't about to argue with me about her decision. "I'm going to find out what happened to Ruby in that motel room!"

"Okay, I promise not to mention it to Daddy. In return for my silence, though, we'll have to stop by Otis Community Center. I want to take a look at the place, get some idea of whether it would accommodate the best anniversary party in the town's history. *That's* my first priority, not Ruby Spikes's death or Sarah Jenkins's tax money."

Mama's shoulders relaxed. "Fine with me," she said, sounding preoccupied.

The Community Center building, one of the largest ones in Otis, is made of precut logs. The hall itself is big enough to hold three hundred people comfortably, and it's a pleasant place, bright and airy. While the Community Center is available for functions like my parents' anniversary party, one of its main uses is for senior citizens' activities. On Saturdays these stately folks get together for a potluck lunch, quilting, knitting, and lots of good gossip. As we arrived, the ladies who made up this week's cleanup crew were putting the last few pots and pans back in the kitchen cupboards. Mama and I greeted them, then I went on into the hall and left Mama behind to chat with her contemporaries.

I looked around, thinking of the party. There was a hardwood floor that was in need of polishing. Stacks of folding chairs were in the corner. Were there enough tables to seat all our guests? We still had to plan the guest list. . . .

Next we drove to Sarah Jenkins's house.

We found Sarah Jenkins, Carrie Smalls, and Annie Mae Gregory once again sitting on Sarah's front porch.

"It's good to see you ladies enjoying the fresh air," Mama commented.

"I need money to pay off my taxes," Sarah said anxiously. "Did you find out anything, anything at all?"

As Mama sat, I swatted a mosquito, then sat on the porch near a rosebush. Its sweet scent filled the air. My mind wandered back to when I was a little girl who believed that time stood still and everything in the world was at peace.

"I'm still looking into it," Mama told her, no doubt feeling that there was more at stake than helping Sarah get Ruby's insurance money.

Now, I've told you before that these three women are the town historians. They know something about every soul who lives in Otis. I knew that Mama counted on them as a source. What I didn't know until today was that they counted on Mama to use their knowledge.

"You've heard that Herman has found Betty Jo dead?" Mama asked, as if she was fairly certain that this news was not going to come as a shock to these women.

From the confident tilt of their heads, I knew that despite Sarah's illness and financial problems, they'd already done some research on Betty Jo's death. And they wouldn't have been satisfied with just listening to the radio or reading the paper. Delight flickered in Carrie Smalls's eyes. She particularly was proud that Mama considered them an important resource. And she for one wouldn't let her down.

"Talk is that Betty Jo and Herman had a knock-down-drag-out fight last night," she said. "I talked to old man Capers, who cleans floors at the morgue. He told me that Betty Jo had fresh bruises on her face and neck when they brought her body in."

"Let me tell you something else I just learned,"

Sarah said. "I got a call this morning from Delcena, the bank teller. She wanted to know how I was doing. During our conversation, Delcena told me that she told Herman that she'd given Ruby a lot of money in cash, and he acted like he didn't care nothing about that."

Mama showed no emotion. Sarah's information was old news to her, since Abe had already told us about his talk with Delcena.

"Delcena told me that she also told Herman that she'd given Ruby most of the money in hundred-dollar bills but that Ruby requested two thousand dollars in twenty-dollar bills," Sarah added.

Now Mama seemed interested. "Ruby got two thousand dollars in twenty-dollar bills?"

"That's what Delcena told me she told Herman," Sarah said, her voice a little stronger, as if she was satisfied that what she said held Mama's interest. "Delcena went on to tell me that she thought it was foolish for Ruby to have had all that money, but then she knew that Ruby wasn't the kind of person you could say that to." She shook her head.

"By the way, Candi." Annie Mae's tone indicated that she wasn't about to be topped by Sarah's news. "I talked to my cousin Christine that lives in Philadelphia. You know I told you I'd ask her to check on Ruby's aunt for you."

"Yes," Mama said politely. "I was hoping you'd receive some news."

"Christine told me that Ruby's aunt Laura died in the old folks' home about three months back. Laura left Ruby an insurance policy worth seven thousand dollars."

Learning that Ruby had received an insurance inheritance was indeed news to Mama. "So, Ruby had seven thousand dollars. Why would she carry that much cash on her person?"

"What I want to know," I interjected, remembering that Abe had told us that there wasn't even a dollar in the motel room where Ruby had been killed, "is what happened to all that money!"

Mama looked at me but didn't respond.

"Somebody killed poor Ruby," Sarah wailed. "There ain't no reason for a woman with all that money to kill herself! Ruby was killed and I won't be able to hold my head up in this town like the respectable woman that I am until I get my tax money and pay my taxes on time!"

Mama didn't say anything but her silence told me that Ruby's death was more important to her than Sarah's reputation.

Supper was over. My father and Cliff were in the backyard, doing what they enjoyed most—drinking cold beer and swapping stories. Mama and I were in the kitchen doing what I liked least—finishing up the dishes. "I've got sample invitations," I told her.

"Young lady, I'll do you one better! I've got a menu and the guest list." She walked over to the desk that sits in a corner of the kitchen, pulled out two neatly typed documents, and handed them to me.

I was more than pleased.

"So, what else do you need from me?" Mama asked, the look on her face saying that she'd finally decided to work with me on whipping this party into shape.

"What about a photographer? We'll need family pictures."

"James's buddy Coal takes pictures for weddings and christenings. James has already spoken to him."

"Your dress?" I asked.

"I've got a few things I can wear."

"You'll need a *new* dress, Mama. Something very chic."

"Okay, I'll buy a dress."

"And Daddy will need a tux," I continued.

"James can rent a tux," she replied, then said, "Simone, have James or I ever made you ashamed by what we had on?"

"No, of course not, Mama," I said quickly.

"Then we'll be fine for the party, I promise you. Let me tell you what I've planned for the entertainment," she said, instantly forgiving me. "James has a buddy who deejays for various functions. James asked him to play music for us."

"Sounds good to me."

"James is going to pick the music, so expect oldies but goodies," she warned me. "So, what else is left to plan?"

"It sounds like we've got everything in order."

"Good," Mama said firmly, walking back to the desk and pulling out a yellow pad and a ballpoint pen. She handed them to me. "Now that we've gotten that settled, I want you to write down what we know about Ruby Spikes's death." I recognized the determined look in her eyes and knew we'd be staying up late. When it comes to being persistent, Mama's a lot like me.

CHAPTER
FOURTEEN

R ight after lunch the next day, Cliff and I left Mama's house for Atlanta. All the while we were driving, I was going over what I still needed to do for the party, but the thought of the two attempts on Mama's life—and on mine—kept coming back to me.

"Cliff," I finally confided. "There is something I need to tell you, but you have to promise not to tell my father."

Cliff looked at me, surprised.

"It's about Mama," I started, then I told him of both the deliberate push into the ditch the week before, and how my mother and I had been shot at at Betty Jo's house and how the cat had been stolen from the backseat of the car.

"Simone! You'd better tell your father—all kinds of bad things can happen to Miss Candi! This game you and your mother insist on playing is getting out of control! Neither you nor your mother are detectives . . . you have no idea of how the criminal mind works!"

"Things usually turn out okay," I reminded him, almost offended by his lack of respect for the positive results of our past investigations.

"There is always the chance that you'll both come out dead!" he snapped, unimpressed. "As soon as you get home, call your father. Tell him that your mother is in danger!"

"But I promised Mama that I wouldn't tell him."

"You need to tell somebody," Cliff insisted.

"I'll call Abe as soon as I get home."

Satisfied that calling Abe and telling him to keep an eye on Mama was the right thing to do, my mind once again wandered to the party. I knew I could count on Cliff and my girlfriend Yasmine and her husband Ernest. They'd all promised to help. Now I gave Cliff his assignment: taking charge of the beverages.

"What kind of liquor do you want to serve?" he asked.

"Beer," I told him. "My father's favorite is Heineken. And wine."

"Nothing else?"

"No," I said. "Select a wine that will go with turkey and ham. The beer will be for Daddy's cronies; they won't know what to do with wine."

"Who's going to serve the liquor?" Cliff asked.

The glint in his eyes told me that he didn't want to be the bartender.

"Ernest offered to tend the bar," I told him.

"You sure you don't want mixed drinks?"

"I'll call and discuss the drinks with my brothers. It'll give me some idea of how much of our budget I should put into liquor."

"When are you going to take everything to Otis?" Cliff asked me.

"I'd like to take the beer and wine home next Saturday."

"I'll go with you again," he said. "Somebody has got to protect you and your mother from yourselves!"

I smiled. "No problem. By the way, Daddy is handling the music."

"Sounds like we're going to be swinging to the oldies."

I laughed. "You can be sure of that!"

"Do you have the Otis Community Center reserved?"

"Yes, but Mama remarked that Lois Eager, the woman who makes the reservations for the center, has a habit of booking two occasions at the same time. So I'm going to give Lois a second *and* a third reminder call." Then I remembered something. "Dinner plates and silverware!" I shouted in poor Cliff's ear. "I've got to find a place to rent dishes and silverware!"

Cliff shook his head. "Honey, there ain't no place

to rent dinnerware or silver within a hundred miles of Otis."

"Then I'll have to rent them in Atlanta and bring them to Otis."

He frowned. "Simone, that sounds like a lot of trouble you're putting yourself through."

"Nothing is too much trouble for my parents' anniversary party. I won't have Mama's guests eat off paper plates. She'd have a fit."

"I have to admit that paper plates ain't Miss Candi's style," he said, nodding.

"Where can I get enough plates—"

"How many people are you expecting?"

"One hundred. That number includes people from out of town, friends my parents have kept in touch with over the years. That means I've got to find a place for all those people to stay." I groaned. Every time I solved one problem, two more cropped up.

"There's the Avondale Inn and the Otis Motel."

"Yes," I said, thinking about Ruby and Betty Jo and how both those places had become a part of Mama's life even before her party.

Once I'd gotten back home and talked with Abe on the phone, I felt like a great weight had been lifted off my shoulders. Abe promised he'd track down Leman Moody and question him and get Rick to keep a close eye on Mama. Now I could get back to planning the anniversary party. I set up a conference call to my brothers. "Are either of you planning on bringing anybody to the party?"

Rodney spoke first. "I'm bringing my new lady and a buddy and his wife."

"Will?" I asked.

"I'm only bringing one lady, somebody I want Mama and Daddy to meet."

"She sounds special," I said.

"She *is* special," Will replied, his tone playfully sensuous.

"You planning to do something serious?" Rodney asked him, sounding a little worried.

"Yeah, big brother," Will said. "I'm going all the way with this one."

"Mama will be glad," Rodney said, not responding to Will's teasing. "I'm sure she's thinking that all three of her children are devoted bachelors who would never give her a grandchild."

"I'm going to get married," I said stoutly.

My brothers both laughed. "Yeah, Simone," said Will, "we know that in about twenty or thirty years Cliff will finally take the plunge—"

"Laugh if you want to," I told them, "but we'll see who strolls down the aisle first."

"Don't worry about beating me to the preacher," Rodney said. "I ain't about to do anything crazy!"

"Let's get back to Mama and Daddy's party," I said sternly, seeing that we were once again headed in the wrong direction. "Now that we've got the party tied down, what are we going to give them as a gift?"

"A gift?" Will echoed. "I thought the *party* was our gift."

"The party is to let everybody see what a great gift we're going to give our parents," Rodney said. "Isn't that right, Simone?"

"Exactly," I said.

"Okay," Will said, like he always does when he sees that Rodney has taken my side, "what kind of gift do you think we should buy?"

"A trip," Rodney said, before I could answer. "A nice long trip."

"You're talking about hundreds of dollars," Will chided. He hates spending money.

"Thousands," I said. "Two thousand at least."

"Not bad," Rodney said.

"The party is costing that much," Will complained.

"Mama and Daddy will only have this anniversary once, and—" I started to say.

But Will cut in. "Simone, spare me the sermon."

"Then you'll agree to a trip?"

"I won't have any money left for my own wedding," Will argued.

"Elope," Rodney said. "Save your cash for the divorce."

"Rodney," I said before my two brothers could start their squabbling, "I'll check on a nice trip, let you know what I can get one for. Then I'll call you back."

"Let Rodney do the calling," Will said abruptly

and rudely. "He's the man who will never get married. He's got the money—"

"If a trip is too much for you, little brother," Rodney shot back, "I'll spring yours for you as a loan, but there will be thirty percent interest to pay."

"I can hold up my end," Will snapped. "Simone, just let me know my share."

"Now, boys," I began.

And maybe I sounded like I was talking down to them, because Will came back with a sharp, "Simone, how big do boys grow in Atlanta?"

"Big enough to send their parents on a trip?" Rodney asked, not letting up on Will's unwillingness to spend another two thousand dollars on a trip for my parents.

"I'll call you both later," I said hastily and hung up the phone. I had so much to do still, and time was running out. My parents' party was in less than a month. This was no time for my brothers to engage in a sibling verbal boxing match. Even though their skirmishes usually turned out innocent fun and soon forgotten, I wasn't in the mood!

CHAPTER

FIFTEEN

By the end of the week, I was exhausted. I had no idea that making arrangements for a party could be such hard work. Oh, I'd had a few get-togethers at my apartment before. But all I did for those was to make a few phone calls, buy pizzas and beer, and let things go with the flow. I'd never done anything as extensive as pulling together this affair for my parents. And I wanted this shindig to be just right—Mama and Daddy deserved the best, and to me, the best meant everything had to be *perfect*.

I was tired but I was satisfied.

I'd ordered invitations, and paid extra money to have them do a rush job for me. The invites needed to be in the mail before the weekend.

I'd also reserved ten rooms at the Avondale Inn and the Otis Motel. I decided that would be a start until I got the RSVPs back. If more people were going to need rooms, there was another hotel thirty miles away in Carrolton. I'd called the reservation clerk at the Carrolton Motel and told her of my plans. She had assured me that September was a slow month and the odds of her having rooms were very good. So I breathed easily, pretty certain that Mama's out-of-town guests would be every bit as comfortable as Mama would want them to be.

I'd called each one of the people on Mama's list who would be coming from out of town. I told them about the party, assured them that an invitation was forthcoming and that arrangements had been made for accommodations. I was pleasantly surprised when each one told me that they'd be glad to attend.

I'd found a place in Atlanta that would rent me dishes and silverware. They reluctantly allowed me to take them out of town to Otis for the party but not without me giving them a three-hundred-dollar deposit check. The check would be returned to me uncashed if there were no broken or lost pieces. Fortunately, Yasmine and Ernest volunteered to be responsible for picking up the dishes, taking them to Otis, and returning them back to the rental service. And Yasmine had already made a breathtaking centerpiece for my parents' table.

I'd checked with several travel agents and had selected a trip to the Caribbean. For two thousand dollars, my parents could take a wonderful cruise to either Jamaica, Barbados, or Martinique.

Friday evening around six o'clock, I'd plopped down on my couch, popped open a diet Coke, and switched on the television. I was expecting Cliff any minute. All we'd planned for the evening was a night of hot wings and a few old movies. (I'd picked up *The Name of the Rose*, starring Sean Connery, a movie that I'd seen before but that I liked, and my favorite James Bond, *The Spy Who Loved Me*, with Roger Moore, and Wesley Snipes's *Passenger 57*.)

The rental car was already packed with chardonnay and Heineken. The next day, we'd deliver all the liquor to Otis and I was to pick up my Honda from the body repair shop where it had spent the past few weeks. My father had insisted that his mechanic work on my car; he swore that this guy was the best in the business. Daddy said that the man would make sure my car was running in tip-top condition again before he'd let me put it on the three-hour trip back to Atlanta.

When the phone rang, I took my time answering it.

"Simone," Mama began without waiting for me to ask why she was calling. "You won't believe what I just learned about Ruby Spikes!"

"What?"

"Do you remember Louise Barker?"

"No."

"Louise is the legal secretary of Calvin Stokes."

"The lawyer who handled Hannah Mixon's will?" Hannah Mixon's death last year was one of the cases Mama and I had helped solve.

"The same," Mama continued, clearly excited with what she was about to tell me. "I ran into Louise at the florist an hour ago. She told me, confidentially of course, that Ruby Spikes had come to Calvin's office to make out a will."

Now Mama had my attention; I sat up straight on the sofa.

The words spilled out of Mama's mouth so fast I thought she was going to lose her breath. "Louise told me Ruby asked Calvin a few questions and then told him she'd come back after she decided on a few things . . . but Ruby never returned!"

"So?"

"So?" Mama said, sounding more than a little annoyed with my reaction, "Ruby made that visit to Calvin's office the day *before* she died!"

"That's interesting," I said. "Why would she ask questions about making a will and then go off and shoot herself?"

"That's the exact same question I've asked myself. And that's not the only thing that's mysterious," she continued. "Sparkle, Curtis and Mack's cat, showed up at Portia Bolton's house. The boys were glad to see their pet, but I can't for the life of me figure who took the poor thing in the first place!"

"And who tried to kill you to get it from you," I said.

"There are so many things going on in Otis."

I agreed, then tried to turn the conversation to the party. Mama listened to my recital of the preparations I'd made, told me, "That's fine, honey," and said good-bye. I knew that what she was really thinking about was the tidbits she'd just learned about the late Ruby Spikes and Betty Jo Mets's cat.

Cliff and I pulled into Otis at noon on Saturday. We unloaded the beer and wine at my parents' house, then went and picked up my Honda, which looked even better than new, and returned the rental car. We got back to Mama and Daddy's house at one o'clock, just in time for lunch.

Though Mama calmly watched us savor her food, I knew her well enough to know that she was anxious to get on with tackling the events that had shaken the serenity of Otis.

When we'd finished our lunch, Mama took me aside and said, "The rapist has struck again. Dawn Crosby was attacked early this morning. This time the man succeeded. The poor girl is in shock; she's been admitted to the hospital." Mama's voice shook; Dawn was the grown daughter of a friend of hers.

"Abe called and asked me if I'd go talk to her," Mama continued. "I said you and I would be there shortly."

"Let me just tell Cliff and then I'll be right with you," I said matter-of-factly, trying not to let on how scared and nervous I felt. I wondered what kind of shape Dawn was in, and I wondered what Mama and I could possibly say or do to help her.

Dawn Crosby was curled up in bed like a little child. I had never been raped, but I knew women who had been where Dawn was at. I wasn't surprised by how miserable she looked. She'd been violated and it showed.

We sat quietly next to her bedside for some time before Mama decided to speak. "Dawn," she began gently. "I know you've been through an ordeal."

At first Dawn stared at us with a blank look, then she buried her face in the pillow. "It was horrible," she wailed.

Mama reached out and touched Dawn gently. "It must have been a nightmare."

Dawn shook her head violently. "I fought as hard as I could," she cried. "Lord knows, I tried to stop him!"

"You did a good job, too," Mama reassured her.

Dawn pulled herself up in the bed. Her eyes darted back and forth from Mama to me, and back again. "I was asleep. I tried to scream, but—" She sobbed.

"I understand from Abe that you got a look at this man."

Dawn shuddered. "When it was all over, I snatched the blanket from my head. I saw him, all right!"

"You say he was young?"

Dawn looked at Mama strangely, like she didn't understand why she was asking questions. "I gave Abe his description," she said.

"Abe told me you think he's about twenty-two or

-three. That he's big, tall, and that all of his hair was shaved."

"That's right."

"You don't remember seeing this man around town?"

Dawn closed her eyes. "I don't know," she whispered. "I don't know anything anymore."

Mama stood up. "We'll let you rest now," she said softly. "I'll be back later. I've got some homemade soup that I think you'd enjoy."

When Dawn looked up at Mama, I could see the tears that filled her terrified eyes, tears that slipped silently down her cheek. "I tried to stop him, Miss Candi," she whispered. "I did everything in my power to stop him!"

Mama pulled Dawn into her arms. "You did the right thing, Dawn," she told her firmly and lovingly. "You did all that you could have done, and that was the right thing to do."

Dawn curled up in Mama's arms and closed her eyes. The only sound that came from her now was a whimper. She reminded me of a puppy, one that was hurt, lost, and very, very afraid.

CHAPTER
SIXTEEN

Cliff and Daddy were gone when Mama and I got back home at three o'clock. Mama seemed tired and withdrawn; she lay down on the couch in the family room and stared up at the ceiling, not saying a word. I understood her mood, so I gave her some space. Around four o'clock, though, I couldn't stand the silence any longer.

"Mama," I started as gently as I knew how, "I know you're thinking about everything that has happened in Otis the past few weeks, but—"

"Simone," she cut in. "My intuition tells me that I know something, but I can't for the life of me figure out what it is."

"Something like what?" I asked.

"Something that will make all that has happened with Ruby, Betty Jo, and Dawn come together."

"You think all three of their experiences are related?"

"I don't know," she admitted. "I feel like I'm on a mountain looking down at shadows."

I got up and followed her to the window, leaning against the wall so that I could see her face. I hated to see Mama like this, like she was bottled up and couldn't figure out how to become unplugged. Her frustration always touched something deep inside of me. Mama was the coach who made our team a winner; I hated to see her disheartened, especially since I didn't have her skill of making lemonade out of lemons.

Just then my father rushed inside the house, his eyes shining with excitement. Cliff was right behind him.

"Candi, baby," my father said, almost out of breath. "I think we've come up with the dude that's been climbing in women's windows and jumping them in their beds!"

A funny feeling rushed through me.

"James," Mama said, "you're not kidding me, now are you?"

Daddy looked Mama straight in the eye. "Baby, would I do something like that?" he exclaimed. "We think we know who he is. We're not sure, but we think—"

"What makes you *think* you've spotted the right fella?"

"For one thing, this guy has fresh scratches all

over his face and neck. I can tell that a woman had hold of him for a good while," Daddy said. "And he's talking crazy, boasting that he scored last night with a woman that he had to make *give* him what he wanted! And Coal now remembers that he's seen this guy wearing a shirt that looked exactly like that piece of cloth you showed us that Ruby had torn from the man who attacked her!"

"This is wonderful," Mama told him. "We've got to get ahold of Abe before we lose this man," she said, walking to the phone and dialing Abe's number. A moment later she hung up with a sigh. "His answering machine is on; he's not in the office," she told us.

"What do we do now?" I asked.

Mama turned to my father. "Do you know the name of this man?"

"Around the pool hall he's called Honey Man. I don't know his given name."

"My Lord." Mama's eyes shone now, her frustration blasted away. "We have to get in touch with Abe!"

"Listen, Candi," Daddy said. "I left Coal at the pool hall to keep an eye on the guy. This is what we're going to do. I'm going back to the hall, just in case Coal needs me. This Honey Man is big. He weighs every bit of two hundred fifty pounds or more. And he's all muscle. I'm surprised that Ruby was able to fight him off as long as she did—truth is, I'm surprised that any woman would be able to fight him at all."

"What do we do?" Mama asked.

"You and Simone go to Abe's office and wait for him."

"I want in on this," Cliff now said.

"You stay here," Daddy told him. "If Abe calls, tell him to get to his office as soon as possible. Tell him that Candi and Simone are waiting there for him."

"Why don't I just call 911?" I suggested.

"If this Honey Man isn't the fella who is climbing into women's bedroom windows, you'd be hard pressed to explain an emergency call," Daddy told me.

Mama nodded resignedly. "James is right," she told me. "Let's do as he says and go to Abe's office to wait."

❧

Abe's office was locked, so Mama and I sat waiting in the car for him. An hour passed before Abe arrived. There was sweat on his face and his shirt was wet and dirty. When he saw us waiting, he ushered us inside his office, closed the door, went behind his desk, sat down, and started fussing. "That darned old man Thrasher who lives next door to Vincent Kelley should have been locked up in the state hospital years ago," he grumbled.

"Mr. Thrasher isn't crazy," Mama told Abe. "The poor old soul is suffering from Alzheimer's disease."

I was impatient to get on with what we'd been

waiting to tell Abe. "This isn't the time to talk about Mr. Thrasher," I said.

Abe ignored me. "I don't care what he's got," he said, annoyed. He pulled out a cigarette and stuck it in his mouth. Then, as if he remembered that he didn't smoke in front of Mama, he snatched it from between his lips and threw it down on his desk. "Thrasher wanders off at least three times a week. His wife, Cassie, expects me and Rick to drop everything and go searching for him. There's a whole lot more to my job than tracking down an absentminded man!"

"Listen," Mama said firmly, giving Abe her most steely-eyed look. "James and Coal think they've identified the man who's been attacking the women in town."

Abe's mouth dropped in amazement. "Who is he and where is he?" he asked.

"His name is Honey Man. He's playing pool at Joe's Pool Hall right this minute. James and his buddy Coal are keeping an eye on him."

Abe stepped into the corridor outside of his office and shouted, "Rick! Come in here! It seems that James may have spotted the rapist."

"James told us that Honey Man is big—if he decides to put up a fight, you'll have a tough one on your hands," Mama warned Abe.

And Mama was right.

Mama and I waited in Abe's office for more than an hour, staring out of the window into the streets of Otis.

We were just about to leave Abe's office when my father arrived.

"I came to tell you to drive your mother home," he told me. "Candi baby, things aren't coming together the way I'd hoped they would."

"What's happened?" Mama asked, instantly concerned. "Did Abe arrest Honey Man? Has anybody gotten hurt?"

"No, no, baby. Nothing like that has happened." Daddy touched Mama's arm. "Do as I say and drive home. I'll meet you there. We'll talk then."

When we got into the house and Mama had made a fresh pot of coffee, Daddy told us this story: The moment Honey Man saw Abe and Rick Martin approaching him, he pulled out a knife. There was a scuffle. Honey Man's eyes were wild, like those of a madman. Other men in the pool hall scattered. Honey Man broke loose from Abe and Rick and used the confusion to push through the crowd and make it through the back door. In a few seconds he was across the street. Abe and Rick followed, but Honey Man was fast. By the time Abe and Rick decided to go back to the pool hall and get their car, Honey Man was no place to be found.

In the middle of the next week, Mama called me in Atlanta to give me the news. Honey Man had been captured. This was Mama's account: Abe and Rick drove around town, telling people that Honey Man was the alleged rapist. But no one knew where he had gone; Honey Man had simply vanished from Otis on Saturday. Then, on Wednesday, Abe and Rick got a tip. Loggers had spotted Honey Man near an old cabin in the woods five miles behind Herman Spikes's place. They surrounded the place and Honey Man was finally captured.

"Are you coming home this weekend?" Mama asked now.

"Yes," I said, remembering that Yasmine had asked me to get her two or three of my parents' wedding pictures. She'd wanted to surprise them by having one of the photos blown up and become part of a special table centerpiece.

"What time Saturday can I expect you?"

"Early."

"Nine o'clock."

"Not that early!" I protested. "It's a three-hour drive!" I took a deep breath. There was no point in resisting her. Mama always got her way. "Okay, pretty lady. I'll be in Otis at nine-thirty Saturday morning," I said, feeling a slight victory because I'd pushed the time back a half hour.

"Tell Cliff I'll have breakfast on the table at *nine* o'clock," Mama replied, her voice soft but resolute. Then she hung up the telephone.

CHAPTER

SEVENTEEN

Saturday evening. The sun hung low in the sky, and the air was heavy with humidity. Silence hung over us like a long, dark cloud.

Mama seemed thoughtful as we drove the twenty miles through the pine tree farm to Avondale.

It had been hard for me to convince Cliff that Mama and I would be safe driving to Avondale alone. If he had, like he'd insisted, taken the drive with us, Mama might have suspected that I'd told him about the attempts on our lives. As it was, she knew about my concerned phone call to Abe—he'd called both me and Mama to report that he'd talked to Leman Moody and that everything would be okay. Mama may not have minded me letting Abe know about our close calls, but she wouldn't have been happy if Cliff or my father started looking after us like guardian angels.

Anyway, I started to put a Sade CD into the car's player, but then I glanced at Mama and decided against it. She looked as if something serious was going on inside her head. I knew not to interfere whenever Mama looked so reflective. It would have been useless anyway.

The truth was, I was sulking. I wasn't happy that Mama seemed so interested in the problems of Otis and so disinterested in her own party. I really wanted to pull out all the stops so that it would be an anniversary both she and my father would always remember. Yet she didn't seem to care much about it one way or the other.

When we arrived at the Avondale Inn, Mama motioned me to park. "I don't want to get out," she told me, glancing down at her watch. "I just want to sit here and try to figure out what really happened to poor Ruby."

I pulled the car onto the grass under a spreading live oak and turned off the ignition. I rolled down the window. Crickets sang; the salty smell of french fried potatoes filled the air. Directly across the street was the McDonald's where we'd had our first meeting with Leman Moody.

I tried to visualize Ruby Spikes, upset, unwanted, alone. And with a wad of money in her purse. So much money, I thought. So little happiness.

We sat until I began fidgeting—I was rapidly getting bored. Mama must have noticed, because she said, "All right, Simone, let's drive back to Otis."

At that moment, Leman Moody, Inez Moore, and a man that I assumed was Inez's boyfriend stepped out of the McDonald's across the street. At first they seemed preoccupied with their conversation, but then Leman spotted us. As he spoke to them, he pointed to us.

"I think," I told Mama, uneasy that I was in the same vicinity as Leman Moody, "that we'll make the trip home faster than we made it to Avondale!" The twenty-mile return trip to Otis took us only fifteen minutes.

"I've got news," was the announcement that Abe hit us with when we got home. He'd been there waiting. "It's official . . . Ruby Spikes did *not* commit suicide. The medical examiner hasn't done Betty Jo's autopsy yet, but his report on Ruby shows that she had minute hemorrhages in her eyelids and throat. She was dead *before* she was shot. Somebody suffocated her, then shot her to make it look like she killed herself. There wasn't any gunpowder on her hands. And the paper that I told you we found in her hand was a piece of a twenty-dollar bill. It looks like somebody killed her for the money that we can't account for," Abe said so fast, he almost didn't take a breath. He was really excited.

Mama started to say something, but Abe held up his hand. "There's more. Rick came up with the idea that the dates and phone numbers that you suggested Jeff Golick pull together for me might put me onto Charles Parker. And he was right. No sooner did I have that list in my hands than I realized that I was onto something. You'll see, Candi, Ruby stayed at the Avondale Inn eight times during the past six months. About three months ago she started making calls to a Savannah number."

Mama's eyes were glued to the list of neatly typed names and numbers that Abe had handed her.

"That number there in Savannah is for a real estate office," Abe said. "The Charles Parker Real Estate Office."

"Ruby was buying property?" I asked.

"I talked to Parker over the phone," Abe said as Mama handed him back the typed list. "He told me he didn't even know that Ruby was dead. He claims the last time he talked with Ruby was four weeks ago."

"Ruby had so many secrets," Mama murmured.

"Parker is coming to my office tomorrow morning around ten," Abe said. His blue eyes blazed with the excitement of finding Charles Parker. "He promised to bring information that will prove his relationship with Ruby was strictly a business one. Still, I ain't taking no chances. I called my buddy, Savannah's chief of police, Adams. He's doing a rundown on Parker for me. He's also having one of his men keep an eye on him for me. If Parker doesn't show up tomorrow morning at ten o'clock here in Otis like he promised, Adams will have him picked up for questioning."

"I'd like to meet Charles Parker," Mama said.

The smell of honey-baked ham told me that Mama had already gotten Sunday dinner well on its way when, at eight-thirty the next morning, I shuffled out of my bedroom into the kitchen.

"Breakfast is light," she said, wiping her hands on her apron. Then she motioned me toward toast, bacon, juice, and peaches. "I'll poach you an egg whenever you're ready."

"I'm ready," I said, pouring a cup of hazelnut coffee. A few minutes later my father and Cliff joined us.

Mama served the poached eggs, then looked around her kitchen. Satisfied that everything was in order, she finally joined us at the table.

"Would you believe," I said, my fork in the air, "that this Parker is a real estate broker? Ruby must have been buying property. She couldn't be selling it: she didn't own any."

"Simone and I are going to be at Abe's office when he talks to this Charles Parker," Mama told my father. "But I'll finish preparing dinner before we leave."

"Miss Candi, may I ask what's for supper?" Cliff asked, his glance lingering on the pots on Mama's stove.

"I've baked a ham."

"I smell it," he said.

"I've made okra and tomatoes and field peas and rice. I've got potatoes boiling to make salad, and"— Mama pointed to a counter on the other side of her stove—"I've got a pan of bread rising for homemade yeast rolls."

"You kneaded bread this morning?" I asked, wondering what time she had gotten out of bed to have all that cooking done.

"No, Simone. I keep dough in the freezer. It's easy to pull it out. It will have risen nicely by the time we get back home from Abe's office."

Cliff's eyes danced excitedly. "I'll watch that bread every second that you're gone," he teased. But it was a statement that I suspected had more truth in it than jest.

Charles Parker was tall, thin. He had a yellow complexion, the color of summer squash. His salt-and-pepper hair was tastefully trimmed. His hands were slender, his fingers manicured. He wore a tailored pin-striped navy blue suit, a perfectly ironed white shirt, and a bright red tie. A gold-plated tie pin shone on it. His shoes gleamed. He smiled graciously. He reminded me of an undertaker.

Abe introduced us, then told Parker that we were close friends of Ruby's. For a second, Parker looked doubtful, but then the lines in his face smoothed. He accepted Abe's offer of a seat. "Ruby first called me about three months ago," he told us. "She'd seen a piece of property I'd advertised in the Savannah Sunday paper. We made arrangements. She came to my office." He opened a manila envelope and pulled out a signed contract. I had a momentary vision of

Ruby Spikes contemplating the purchase of a house without her husband's knowledge, and wondered just how angry that might have made Herman Spikes.

"Ruby was a good businesswoman," Mama commented.

Charles Parker's manner, which up to now had been detached and coolly professional, softened. "I admired her financial sense," he agreed. "I, of course, guided her. She paid thirty-four thousand dollars toward the purchase of a house. Because of the need of repairs, she struck a good bargain.

"The property was on a one-acre tract in Bartow," Parker continued, showing us a color photograph of a small brick house. "The old woman that owned this house died about six months ago. Her children live up north. They wanted to sell the place quickly, so even though they wanted seventy-five thousand for it, when Ruby offered sixty thousand, they accepted."

Abe was still looking through the papers Parker had handed to him. "Why this check for five thousand dollars?" he asked.

"Ruby asked me to see to the repairs," Parker replied. "That's not usually a part of my duties, but she insisted she had no other resource. The check she gave me paid for new plumbing and wiring."

Abe seemed satisfied that Charles Parker's story was legitimate. "Do you have an idea who might have wanted to kill Ruby?" he asked.

Charles Parker looked Abe in the eyes without blinking. "I do not," he said. "My only dealings with Ruby Spikes were pure business."

"Ruby Spikes's death is an official murder investigation," Abe told Parker.

Charles Parker's face clouded briefly. "I understand," was his soft reply. I could see that he was shaken by Abe's news.

"I'll be getting back with you," Abe continued.

"I'll make myself available," Parker answered as he stood to leave. "Those papers," he continued, "are copies. They're yours to keep. I have the originals in safekeeping."

Charles Parker turned to Mama, looked down at her with genuine interest, and then bowed stiffly. "I'm sorry about Ruby Spikes's untimely death," he said stoically as if he was giving Mama his condolences. Then his voice changed. I swear it even sounded a bit sad. "It was a nice little house. Ruby seemed truly happy with her purchase."

Mama didn't say anything but I could tell from the way she looked at Charles Parker that she believed his assessment.

"Well, Candi," Abe said once Charles Parker was out of his office, "what do you think about all this?"

"I suppose you know for sure that Parker is telling the truth about buying the house? And that the five thousand dollars was for repairs, not for some kind of blackmail payments?"

"I got a call this morning from Chief Adams, in

Savannah. He assured me that Parker's establishment is legitimate, all right."

Mama allowed a long silence. "Let's go," she murmured to me, her eyes once again betraying frustration.

CHAPTER
EIGHTEEN

Thirty minutes after we left the sheriff's office, we pulled off onto a dirt road that wove through a pecan orchard. We drove until the main road was out of sight, leaving clouds of dust. Finally we arrived at a cinder-block house with a rusted tin roof. Chickens pecked in the dirt of the front yard. I beeped the horn. Herman Spikes came through his front door.

Now, I'd heard so much about Herman Spikes that I was almost bowled over when I finally saw the man. While he was about as tall as me, his body was irregularly proportioned, with short arms, a very long torso, and a neck the size of a tree stump. He had a scraggly beard that needed to be trimmed. He wore glasses—thick lenses with a heavy plastic frame. His hair was uncombed and badly in need of a cut. He had on a pair of khaki pants and a yellow shirt that looked as if they hadn't been washed in weeks. And he was drunk. When he stumbled down the wooden steps of his front porch toward us, I thought he was going to fall flat on his face, but he somehow recovered his balance and came to a stop in front of my car.

"Miss Candi," he said, extending a hand to Mama as she climbed out of the car. His voice came out as a deep rasp.

"I'm sorry I didn't come sooner," Mama said courteously, taking his outstretched hand and shaking it.

Herman invited us into his house. It was hot inside; the window air conditioner wasn't turned on. Although the room was smartly furnished in peach and burgundy, it was clear that it hadn't been cleaned for weeks. Everything smelled of whiskey, cigarettes, and sour musk. If Betty Jo had enjoyed Ruby Spikes's house, she'd done little in her housekeeping to prove it.

"I couldn't help but wonder," Mama began, once we'd been seated, "whether or not you suspected that Betty Jo wasn't feeling well that night, before you went to bed."

Herman rocked back on his heels. "You're asking me questions, huh?" he said. I could see that his eyes were bloodshot. "If there weren't so many spiteful people in this town talking things they don't know nothing about," he slurred, his big hands trembling. He paused as if he was trying to remember what Mama had asked him. "Betty Jo was healthy as a horse—never complained of anything." Then, as if he'd just decided that he should do something more, he urged, "Go in there and see where she slept!"

I wasn't surprised when Mama accepted his invitation and walked into his bedroom. Herman stumbled behind me as I followed her.

The room was beautifully decorated. A full-length mirror stood in one corner. There was a writing desk with a cushioned chair. The four-poster bed that I assumed Betty Jo had died in was king sized, with a dark mahogany headboard. All the bedding had been stripped from the mattress.

Herman leaned against the bedpost, looking bewildered. "Miss Candi, I don't know. When I found her, she looked like she was dreaming."

The closet door was open. From where I was standing, I could see dresses, blouses, and jackets. Thrown haphazardly on the floor in a heap were shoes. There was a garment bag. I wondered whether or not Betty Jo had had a chance to try on everything in Ruby's closet.

"I slept good myself," Herman continued. "But I told Abe that Betty Jo was having trouble getting to sleep, that she took something, that whatever she took helped her 'cause when I got up to go to the bathroom I heard Betty Jo snoring. I remember that, all right."

"I suppose Abe told you that he'd finally gotten the autopsy on Ruby."

Herman's eyes blinked rapidly. "I told Abe and I'm telling you. I don't know nothing about Ruby dying! I was locked up in the Otis Motel with Betty Jo that whole night!"

"I know," Mama said, stepping into the adjoining bathroom. I stayed close behind her. Towels, wash-cloths, and clothes were tossed all over the floor.

Suddenly Herman's eyes flickered toward the clothes on the bathroom floor. His expression changed, like he was ashamed of the mess we were looking at. He stepped in front of Mama and mo-tioned us back toward the living room. I was sur-prised at how calm and deliberate he now seemed, as if he was sober. "I don't know what's come over me," he said apologetically. "A bedroom ain't no place to entertain women who came to pay their last respects to the dead!"

Mama studied him for a moment in silence, then she turned and headed out of the room. "I suppose you're right," she agreed.

We said good-bye to Herman Spikes, who didn't bother to hide his relief at seeing us go.

"Why are we going to Susy Mets's house?" I asked Mama as I drove back toward Otis, following Mama's directions.

"Susy is Betty Jo's next of kin. She'll be the one to handle the funeral arrangements. And I've got a spe-cial fondness for Susy. She was one of my first cli-ents when I started working as a case manager. When we talked, I learned that she had the ambition of becoming a medical assistant in a doctor's office.

142

So I set up classes for her through Otis Technical and I got her an apprenticeship with Dr. Huggins. Susy finished school and became one of the nurses Dr. Huggins uses at his office. She also volunteers to help at the health department on Wednesday evenings when working mothers take their children in for their immunization shots."

"She sounds like an okay lady."

"Believe me, she's nothing like her cousin Betty Jo."

"How many children does she have?"

"Two," Mama told me. "Twin girls, Joy and Jane. They're in the fourth grade now and they're doing very well in school."

"You sound like you keep up with the family."

"Susy has so much going for her, and her girls show all signs of having ambition like their mother." Mama sounded proud.

"Mama, I know you're going to pay your respects to Susy because of Betty Jo's death, but I also know that you want to get information from her. What do you want?"

"As closely as I've worked with Betty Jo as her case manager, she just never impressed me as the kind of woman who needed anything to help her sleep," Mama said thoughtfully.

Susy Mets's front yard sported four pine trees, two crape myrtles, and four smaller shrubs.

Susy herself was a tiny woman with a warm man-

ner I liked instantly. She greeted us cheerfully when
we walked up onto her porch. "I'm so glad to see
you, Miss Candi," she said, motioning us to come
inside her home. The house was very cold. I could
hear the air conditioner churning away in the dim-
ness. Susy fumbled with the light, finally turning on a
fringed lamp. I sat in an overstuffed armchair. Susy
sat on a matching couch and Mama sat next to Susy.

"I'm sorry about Betty Jo," Mama told Susy.

"I never thought she'd die in her sleep," Susy told
us, shaking her head. "I mean, the way she lived, I
just never expected her to go to bed and not wake
up."

"Will you have a problem with Betty Jo's burial?"
Mama asked Susy. "There are some county funds
available."

There were tears in Susy's eyes. "I kept a small
policy on Betty Jo, the same as I've got on me and
my girls.

"I wish Betty Jo wouldn't have been the kind of
woman that she was," Susy went on. "I tried hard to
talk her into making something of her life, but she
wouldn't listen to me. Betty Jo wasn't a bad person.
She did good things for people, was always feeding
stray cats and dogs. She even kept the churchyard
clean, made sure there wasn't any paper or trash
left after service. And she helped the old ladies at
the Community Center sew patches for their quilts.
Ask any of them—they'll tell you that Betty Jo did
whatever was needed. She just had a weakness, one

that, at times, made her forget that her boys needed her."

Mama reached out and gently patted Susy's hands. "I know that Betty Jo didn't want to hurt anybody. Unfortunately, the only persons she really did harm to was those boys, Curtis and Mack."

Susy looked up at Mama, a tear spilling down her cheek. "I wish I could have kept the boys. Fact is, it takes all I can do to take care of my girls."

"And you do a good job at it, too," Mama reassured her. "Susy, I need to ask you something about Betty Jo."

"What do you want to know, Miss Candi?"

"Did she ever speak to you about Herman?"

"No, I don't recollect her saying anything about Herman, but then you know he'd only been messing with Betty Jo a few weeks."

"Do you remember exactly when Herman started taking up time with Betty Jo?" Mama asked.

"Let me think. . . . It was about a week before Ruby was killed."

Mama looked surprised.

"There is one thing that Betty Jo told me," Susy said as if it was an afterthought. "Betty Jo was scared of the dark. She tried to tell me something about dreaming that she woke up in the motel room upset because Herman had turned out all the lights. Before she finished telling me her dream, Herman came and stood next to her. After our conversation, Herman wouldn't let Betty Jo out of his sight." She shook her head again. "That's around when she moved into his place. I don't know how long that was going to work, though. My cousin wasn't for sticking too close to any one man for very long."

Mama took a deep breath. "It will be a week before the medical examiner will release Betty Jo's body so that you can have a funeral. Once that happens, if you need help in making funeral arrangements, I'll be glad to be there for you."

Susy's face lit up when she smiled. "Miss Candi, you've already done so much for me. I really can't imagine how I could ever repay you for all of your kindnesses. You taught me so much. What you said about setting goals has helped me to turn my life completely around. I've got so many things I want to do, so many things I want for me and my girls."

Mama looked into Susy's eyes. Her fondness for this young woman was clear. "Your attainment of all those goals is all the thanks I will ever need," she told Susy.

CHAPTER
NINETEEN

Sunday before noon the telephone rang. Mama answered it. When she returned to the table she told us that Sarah Jenkins had called to tell her that she just remembered something that might help find the person who killed Ruby.

"I suppose Sarah's memory is working up to speed now that Ruby's death has been ruled a homicide rather than a suicide," I said.

Mama nodded. "Yes, it means that she can collect on that insurance policy she's been paying on for years."

"More importantly," I sniggered, "the respectable Miss Jenkins will be able to pay her taxes on time, which will stop the townspeople from talking about how silly she was to send her tax money off to Canada on a scam."

Mama smiled and nodded. "In a small town like

Otis, people talking about you can slap you in the face every day. It's a shame that talk can have such a sting, but in Otis it's more like a sore that keeps getting irritated until it festers."

"Sarah can give it but she can't take it," Daddy said.

"Isn't that the way it always works," Mama responded.

"Payback is hell!" I said.

"Sarah Jenkins has got a lot more payback coming to her than what she's just gone through," Daddy said. "That woman, along with her two comrades, has dragged more people's names in the mud than anybody in this town."

"Sarah, Carrie, and Annie Mae got their reputation," Mama agreed. "Still—"

"Mama likes to keep them as her source," I cut in.

"Simone, James and I have been away from this town for thirty years. There is a lot of history that I just don't know."

"Well, teaming up with the good Sarah Jenkins, Annie Mae Gregory, and Carrie Smalls was the right thing for you to do," I said. "They know more about the history of this town than the CIA."

Mama smiled. "They've been helpful in the past."

"Enough about the town's gossips," Daddy said. "I've been thinking about Herman Spikes."

"What about Herman?" Mama asked.

"Candi, you're the one with the suspicious mind in this family, but I can't help but think how unexpectedly Betty Jo Mets died. Now we know that

Ruby was killed. Wouldn't it be something if Betty Jo was murdered too?"

"I've given that a lot of thought," Mama admitted. "I've been Betty Jo's case manager for better than two years now, and I never dreamed she'd go to bed and not wake up. She was a character, so full of life. To be honest, she was too full of life. It's the reason I had to do what I did. She left her two young boys home alone for hours, sometimes days. Things got so bad six months ago that we had to make a decision whether or not to place the boys in a foster home. We held a hearing. Betty Jo answered the hearing officer's questions so honestly, I felt embarrassed for her."

I shrugged. "Betty Jo had reason to be honest at the hearing, Mama. She knew that if the state took those children, she'd be free to do as she pleased."

Mama shook her head. "Simone, I don't think so. First of all, the boys' removal meant that Betty Jo would no longer receive either a welfare check or food stamps. Also, I believe Betty Jo really did love her boys. Trouble is, she loved men, too. And that's exactly what she told the hearing officer. She admitted that she had a weakness for men. That when she had the urge to go with one, she forgot about her boys. She claimed that's why she left them alone too long."

"She was sick," I said.

"She had a problem, yes," Mama agreed. "But Betty Jo was honest enough to admit it. Herman was lucky when he decided to spend the night with Betty

Jo the night that Ruby was killed. Betty Jo had her faults, but the one thing she was known for was being truthful. It was almost like she never learned how to tell a lie."

"So, when she told Abe that Herman had spent the night with her at the Otis Motel, she was telling the truth?" Cliff asked.

"Yes," Mama told him. "If Herman wasn't in that room that night, Betty Jo would have said so!"

"So, her death has no effect on Herman's alibi?" I asked.

"I don't think so," Mama said. "I really don't think so."

Sarah Jenkins opened her front door dressed in a beige two-piece suit, a silk scarf, and a pair of pink slippers; brown one-inch-heel pumps were sitting just inside the door frame.

"Come on in, ladies," she said, ushering me and Mama toward the back of the house. We followed her through the living room, the dining room, and into a short hall that led into a large bedroom. The room had a king-sized white wrought-iron bed in the middle of the floor. A multicolored bedspread covered the bed. On top of it were stacks of old *Otis County Guardian* newspapers.

"I got up this morning determined to go to Sunday school," she told us. "I'm still weak but this is something I begged the good Lord to help me do. It came to me right in the middle of the lesson." She picked up a newspaper from the top of the stack. It was faded yellow. She handed it to Mama, who read the front page silently, then passed it to me.

OTIS COUNTY GUARDIAN
June 10, 1985

OTIS SHOOTING DEATH BEING INVESTIGATED

The Otis Sheriff Department and Otis County Coroner are investigating a shooting death. Coroner Rhoden Black said Laura Manning, 50, of Otis County, died from a self-inflicted single gunshot wound to the head. Manning had last been contacted by telephone by a friend around 10:30 P.M. the night before.

No final ruling has been made in the death but officials do not suspect foul play. Manning's body has been sent to Charleston for autopsy.

Sarah's mouth was set the way it is when she feels she's absolutely correct. "See, Candi," she said, "it's happened before, right here in Otis." She pointed at the newspaper.

Mama looked at Sarah in bewilderment. "I don't understand what you're getting at, Sarah."

Sarah took a breath, then let it out dramatically. "Abe thought Laura Manning killed herself too. But it wasn't so and I was the one who proved it."

Now there was a look of intense interest on Mama's face.

"It was about twenty years ago," Sarah began. "Laura Manning, Annie Mae, Carrie, and I were members of the same chapter of the Eastern Stars. Laura was a widow woman, a fine mother who had raised three children. She worked hard at the church, helped raise money for the youth group's field trip to the Six Flags amusement park in Atlanta.

"Early one morning before daylight a man slipped into Laura's house, threw a blanket over her head, and raped her. Laura reported it to Abe, who did what he could to find the man. Telling Abe about her ordeal wasn't all that Laura did. She talked about it to anybody who'd listen to her. She told the story over so many times that folks started saying she made them feel like they were in that bed of torment with her.

"Three weeks after Laura was raped, the county fair opened in Avondale. Annie Mae, Carrie, and I were taking our time strolling through the fair-grounds, looking at the exhibitions, when we ran into Laura. Like always, Laura started telling us about being raped in her own bed. Then out of the blue she said to us, 'I think I know who raped me!' I tell you, Candi, the look on that woman's face was real strange: like a bolt of understanding had struck her. 'I've got to find Abe and tell him something,' she said, and she hurried away from us without another word.

"The next morning," she added grimly, "I found Laura's body."

"You were the friend the newspaper mentioned," Mama said.

Sarah nodded. "I'd called Laura after I got home from the fair to ask to borrow one of her pans. Laura always kept such nice baking pans. She mentioned to me that she hadn't been able to locate Abe, but first thing the next morning she was going to his office. She said she was sure she had a strong idea of who had crawled through her window."

"And right after that, she supposedly killed herself, is that right?" Mama asked.

"Like I told you, I found her body the next morning when I went to pick up her pan."

"Did Laura Manning leave a note?" I asked before Mama could respond.

"She sure did," Sarah told me. "In Laura's own handwriting were the words *I can't go on!*"

"That's all the note said?" I asked, surprised at its brevity.

"That's it," Sarah said firmly. "Carrie, Annie Mae, and I told Abe what Laura had told us that day at the fair, but it didn't do any good. The coroner ruled that Laura killed herself. He said he based his decision on the fact the gun was in her hand, she had written a note, and she'd been obviously upset over the rape because she wouldn't stop talking about it.

"But now look at this here," Sarah said, handing Mama another newspaper clipping.

OTIS COUNTY GUARDIAN
November 9, 1985

BURNS IS FOUND GUILTY OF MURDER

An Otis County man, Freddy Burns, 38, was found guilty Wednesday of the June 9, 1985, murder of Laura Manning.

The Otis County jury deliberated only four hours before convicting Burns. The trial has now entered the penalty phase, and the jury will decide whether Burns should be put to death or serve a life prison term. Assistant District Attorney John Everritt told jurors Tuesday that Burns should be executed.

Mama's eyes shone with interest. "Tell me about it."

Sarah looked pleased that she had Mama's ear.

"Laura Manning knew Freddy Burns all of her life. When Freddy was a boy, he used to come to their place and help her father clean out his hog pens. But Laura didn't like Freddy. She called him 'trash' in front of his face and behind his back.

"Out of pure spite, Freddy crawled into her window and raped her. He thought that by throwing a blanket over Laura's head, she wouldn't have known who he was. And for a while, she didn't. The way the prosecutor figured it was, as we were standing by the livestock exhibit at the county fair, a particular smell stirred Laura's memory. It probably was the smell of that prize hog she was looking at. I testified at the trial that I saw Freddy Burns standing nearby while Laura was talking to us. I think he must have overheard some of our conversation.

"Laura left the fair but she wasn't able to get ahold of Abe. Sometime during the night, Freddy Burns slipped into Laura's bedroom. He made her write that note. The scoundrel shot Laura in the head, then put the gun in her hand to make it look like she'd killed herself."

"And he almost got away with it?" Mama asked, looking down at the paper in her hand.

"Yes. And he would have if it wasn't for Laura's ballpoint pen."

"Go on," Mama said.

"Laura had a gold ballpoint pen that had a tiny angel on the top of the cap. She loved that pen. She'd picked it up on a visit to her sister in New Jersey. She was particularly proud that nobody in Otis owned one like it. Now, Candi, you know I've got an eye for seeing things that ain't quite right. You can imagine my surprise when, two weeks later, I saw Freddy Burns using Laura's pretty little gold pen with the tiny angel on its cap to write out a money order at the post office."

"What did you do?" Mama asked.

"I hurried to Annie Mae and Carrie and told them exactly what I'd seen. Together the three of us we went straight to Abe. At first he didn't want to pay us any attention. But we wouldn't let him alone until he looked into how Freddy got ahold of Laura's ballpoint pen. Abe got a warrant and searched Freddy's house. He found a pair of Freddy's shoes that matched prints that were found under Laura's window where her killer had been standing.

Mama stared as if Sarah had just given her an electric shock.

"What's wrong?" Sarah asked, touching her own face, her throat.

Mama didn't answer.

I understood. My mother's mind was working, things were beginning to make sense, pieces were falling into place. "What do you know that I don't know?" I asked, ignoring Sarah's apparent confusion.

Mama stood, nodded good-bye to Sarah, and headed for the door.

I followed.

Once we were seated in the Honda, she told me, "I see the face of the shadow."

CHAPTER
TWENTY

Sunday afternoon in Otis County feels like the region is posing for a talented artist whose giant hand sketches its portrait. The stillness affects everything, including the animals, who move so slowly you'd think they know it's the Sabbath. The quiet is so profound, it's almost hypnotic. Nobody ever thinks of disturbing it.

Today, however, Mama was out of step with Otis's rhythm. She moved not like the turtle, but like the proverbial hare. It was clear that she'd spotted something.

We left Sarah Jenkins's house a little before one o'clock. Mama was enthusiastic. "Simone, I know who killed Ruby, but I've got to get evidence to prove it. Let's go see Jeff Golick. I need to talk to him before I can go any further."

Our drive to Avondale took us along the same de-

157

serted road where we'd almost gotten killed. This trip was infinitely less threatening and yet my mother didn't talk to me. I understood what was going on inside her head so I wasn't upset. Instead, I used the time to search my own memory.

Ruby's murder, Betty Jo's untimely death, the rapist Honey Man—they were all pieces of a puzzle. Try as I might, however, I couldn't recollect anything to help me understand it.

Jeff Golick was in his office. Mama knocked gently and he invited us in. He was sitting in a swivel chair behind a desk stacked with what looked like receipts. When he looked up, impatience settled in his face. "I can't believe you've come back to bother me again. What do you want *now*?"

"I'm sorry to disturb you," Mama explained calmly, as if she didn't see his annoyance, "but I must have a description of the scarf Ruby wore around her neck the last Friday night she checked into the Inn. Can you make me a drawing of it?"

The expression on the manager's face altered to one of disbelief. Then he started to look obstinate, but finally he cleared his throat and sighed in resignation. He found a clean sheet of paper among those on his desk and gave the drawing his best shot. When he'd finished, he handed what he'd done to my mother.

Mama's face brightened. "This is wonderful! Thank you! And once again I'm sorry to have bothered you," she told him, as she signaled me to leave.

Jeff Golick's eyes rolled toward the ceiling as his wave dismissed us.

Once we were outside of his office, Mama's gaze lingered on the design for what seemed like a long time.

I looked over her shoulder. "What do you see in that kindergarten drawing?" I asked, since the sketch didn't look like anything to me.

"I see what confirms my suspicion, but before I can be completely sure, I need to make two phone calls."

"There are telephones down the street, near the McDonald's."

We drove to where Mama made her calls. I sat in the car with my window rolled down. Mama talked on the phone.

Out of a corner of my eye, I saw Inez Moore and the big fella who I'd seen her with previously. Neither saw me. They were on their way to the drive-thru. When Inez's eyes did lock with mine, they sent me a dagger of a message: she'd love to fight me just as she'd fought Ruby in the factory's parking lot.

Inez muttered something to her companion, who turned and sent me an equally evil stare. Then the man seemed to decide against hamburgers. He pulled out from the drive-thru onto the highway. The look Inez sent me reminded me of how angry she was, how there was no way she'd feel pain, remorse, or regret for anything she'd ever done to poor Ruby Spikes.

Mama eased inside the car. "Things are all set up. I called Abe and got the phone number of Kip Barker, the manager of the garment factory where Ruby worked. Mr. Barker's given us permission to visit him at his home."

Mama was as quiet on this trip as she'd been on the drive to Avondale. For the first time since we'd last visited Sarah, I thought about the anniversary party. I was wise enough to realize that this wasn't the time to discuss it. Folks, I have to tell you I had another reason to be glad she'd reached this point in solving Ruby's murder: By the time we'd be ready to celebrate, the killer would be locked up and we'd finally have Mama's undivided attention!

Kip Barker lived in the same town as Leman Moody. His house was off of a dirt road that wove through a grove of willow trees draped in shawls of moss. The house was a one-story pale green stucco. The lot was large and nicely landscaped. A red Ford was parked in the concrete driveway and an old Nissan sat on the grass on the side of the yard.

On the porch, we knocked, and waited for an answer. The man who answered the door was in his mid-sixties, with a mix of gray-and-white hair and a thick, white mustache. His complexion was the color of caramel candy. He was wearing cutoffs, a white T-shirt, and a pair of loafers. He greeted us like he really didn't mind our intruding on his Sunday afternoon.

"I'm sorry to bother you," Mama began, "it's just

that this matter of Ruby's death has taken on an urgency."

"I can't imagine what could be so urgent on the Lord's Day, but I wasn't doing anything that I couldn't give you a few minutes."

Mama pulled out the sketch she'd gotten from Jeff Golick. "I need to know whether or not Ruby had recently worked on a scarf like this one."

The manager's eyes rested on the drawing with interest.

Mama went on. "The scarf I'm interested in would have been reddish-brown, cinnamon colored. And the line running horizontally through it would have been slate blue."

Kip Barker was silent.

"It was a wool blend, perhaps with a little rayon," Mama added, as if trying to prime his memory.

Recognition flashed in the manager's eyes. "It's the last lot we shipped for the winter season."

"Did Ruby work on that order?"

He hesitated. "I reckon."

"Are you sure?"

"Yes, I'm sure. Now that I think of it, Ruby asked permission to take two scarves home with her."

"Did you give her the scarves?"

"Not right then, I didn't. I told her to wait. She probably took them on the Friday after the shipping department sent the order."

Mama gave the plant manager a warm smile. "Thank you so very much," she told him, as she shook his hand gratefully. "I do hope you enjoy the remainder of your Sunday afternoon."

"Don't plan to do nothing," Mr. Barker responded as we walked out off his porch.

I glanced at Mama as I turned the key into the Honda's ignition. The euphoric look on her face had intensified. "Where to now?"

"Betty Jo's house."

The front door of the house Betty Jo had occupied before she moved in with Herman Spikes was unlocked, the wooden screen door unhooked. I've already told you that Betty Jo's house was junky. Well, this time it was downright filthy. The bedroom had clothes thrown all over it; the bed was unmade, no big surprise there. The bathroom smelled of urine and mildew. And the kitchen had dirty dishes and garbage everywhere.

The first thing Mama wanted to see was where I'd picked up the rag in which I'd wrapped Sparkle. I showed her the corner of an old chair. As she examined the spot, she picked up pieces of fibers and tucked them into her wallet. When she'd finished, she asked me to help her search the whole place.

"What are we looking for?"

"Money."

I must have made a startled noise, because Mama said, "We're looking for the balance of the two thousand dollars that was in Ruby's motel room when she was killed."

"What makes you think it's here?"

"Portia Bolton told us that Betty Jo gave each of

her sons a twenty-dollar bill, bills that looked like they'd just come off the printing press. If my thinking is correct, Betty Jo got those twenties from this house. I'm hoping that the person who put that money here hasn't yet had the presence of mind to move any more of the money."

We spent the next forty-five minutes searching every nook and cranny in the house. I was pawing through a jumble of old dresses, socks, pants, and skirts when I found a few pieces of torn paper. I started to push them aside when a name caught my eye. *Leman Moody*. It was written on a scrap that had been torn from a bigger piece of paper.

"Mama, look at this!"

I handed my mother what I'd discovered. She looked at it closely, then began going carefully through the pile of things I'd been examining. Finally, she unearthed a whole collection of torn scraps, all of the same kind of paper Moody's name had been scrawled on.

"Simone, help me try to put this back together," she urged.

We played jig-saw puzzle with the pieces of paper until we had put enough of it together. We'd found one of Leman Moody's gambling IOUs—one that had been paid by Ruby Spikes only a week before she was killed. The look on Mama's face told me she understood how the receipt fit into the big picture. She placed the note in her purse.

It was almost four-thirty when we'd gone through everything in the little house. We didn't find money.

As a matter of fact, we didn't even find loose change. Mama's face had clouded. Disappointed, she suggested we go home. But as we started to leave, her face brightened again.

"We didn't look outside of the house," she said.

I followed her as we slowly walked around the front of the house, looking for a place where a person could hide a sum of money.

Nothing.

We started toward the back when Mama spotted an old Mercury at the edge of the yard. "It might be in that," she said. "Get a stick so that we can test the grass around it. We don't want our search to end up with a snake bite."

I used the handle of a discarded mop to jab through the thick grass. After a few minutes, it seemed that there was nothing creepy or crawly in the vicinity.

Then, Mama, who'd already walked around to the passenger's side, opened the door. I pulled on the latch to the door on the driver's side and peered inside. The seats were covered with cat hair.

The floor in the back netted us one of Charles Parker's business cards. Mama glanced at the card with curiosity, then added it to the collection she was storing in her purse.

I was beginning to doubt that we'd find any money. The signals I was picking up from Mama's body language told me she might have been thinking the same thing. She checked the glove compartment, which was crammed with old, stained documents.

I'd laid the mop across the front seat. After she'd closed the glove compartment, Mama reached for the old mop handle and used it to fish underneath the seat of the car.

Folks, it was then that Mama hit pay dirt. The lady pulled out a brand-new, shiny metal box, the kind people around Otis used to keep their important papers and their money in.

"This is it! This is what I'm looking for!"

"*Now* will you share what you've discovered with me?"

Mama shook her head. "Not until I've figured a way to bring a murderous shadow into the light."

CHAPTER

TWENTY-ONE

For an hour after we got back to our house, Mama didn't say anything more. Instead, she rushed into the kitchen and began to pull out her baking utensils with such fury that I understood her silence.

She was planning and she didn't want to be disturbed. Whenever she puts such energy in her baking, oblivious to anything or everybody else, I know that she's using her cooking skills to think—it's an efficient way that works for her.

I made a pot of chocolate almond coffee, deciding that it would go well with whatever comfort food she was throwing together. Then I joined my father and Cliff in the backyard to wait for the results of both her baking and her thinking.

When the tantalizing smell of bread pudding wafted out to us, I knew we'd be in for a treat. Mama makes bread pudding to die for.

Then she summoned us into the kitchen. But before we could be seated, we heard the doorbell.

"I'll get it," Mama said as she hastily moved toward the front door.

When she returned, Abe and his deputy, Rick Martin, were with her. "I called Abe and Rick," she told us. "It's important that they agree to work with us on this."

Then she told the five of us how she'd figured out who had killed Ruby and how she planned to get him to show his hand.

My father jumped up from his chair like a grasshopper. "Candi, your behind will be grass and that man will be a lawn mower!"

From the look on Mama's face, she didn't find my father's analogy amusing. "James," she shot back, "I'm not going to get hurt and you've got to believe that!"

Daddy shook his head. "But why do you want to be the cheese in the rat trap?"

"It's the only way to get the killer to show his hand."

"There is no way I'm gonna let this happen!" my father shouted as he began pacing the floor. "My wife is not going to sit in a chair and let a maniac take a shot at her!"

"He's not going to shoot me," Mama insisted. "Abe and Rick will have him handcuffed before he—"

"Shoots you the second time," my father interrupted. "Candi, baby, please be reasonable. You are not the cavalry . . . this is not your war!"

"It's the only way to get the man who killed Ruby to show his hand," she insisted.

"Abe," Daddy said, "tell my wife that she shouldn't do this!"

Abe's forehead wrinkled and he cleared his throat. "I've already come to the conclusion that even if I tried to get Candi to change her mind, she wouldn't listen to me."

My father shook his head and turned toward me and Cliff. "Cliff! Simone!" he pleaded, his voice and eyes begging for our help in changing Mama's mind.

Cliff didn't move—apparently he'd become dumbfounded by what my mother had just proposed.

"Daddy," I said, seeing that my boyfriend wasn't going to be any use to us at the moment, "what do you think about me being the bait in Mama's plan?"

"No you won't," Mama said before my father had a chance to say anything. "This is not a matter to be pulling straws over. I'm confident that if everybody does what they are supposed to do, I won't get hurt."

"Let Abe or Rick sit in the chair," my father urged. "It's their job to trap killers. You've done enough already!"

"Ruby's killer will be expecting to see a woman's shadow," Mama said. "If Abe or Rick sit as bait, he'll become suspicious."

My father's right hand pounded the kitchen table with such force that everything on it shifted. "I ain't gonna let you do it! There's no need to talk about it anymore."

"James," Mama said in her usual warm, confident

tone, "you know that I'm not a woman to take un-
necessary chances. That's why I want you close to
me. With you close by my side, I know everything
will work out fine."

Daddy's face didn't lose its obstinacy as he walked
over to the window and gazed out of it in silence.

I took a deep breath. I couldn't help but wonder
how my father would react if he knew that this would
be the third time Mama had sat like cheese to this
particular rat. As it was, I'd hardly ever seen him this
upset. Still, I realized that despite my father's plead-
ing, Mama hadn't changed her mind. I decided to
intercede. "Daddy," I said, joining him at the window, "Mama's plan will work if we see to it that the
rat is caught before he snatches her."

My father turned to face me. "Simone honey, your
old man has looked more than one killer in the eyes.
I ain't never been accused of losing my cool under
fire, but I ain't so sure that I can just sit there quietly
while a murderer takes a shot at your mother."

Mama walked over and put her arms around my
father. "James, I promise—nothing is going to happen to me."

Daddy stepped back and threw up his hands in
disgust. "Okay, okay! So now, after thirty-five years
of what I considered a decent marriage, you're telling me that you, my wife—the mother of my children—is Superwoman!"

The silence became thick; for what seemed like an
eternity nobody said anything more.

Finally my father looked into Mama's eyes. His

shoulders slumped, his voice lowered. "Candi baby, I don't want you to do this, but if you insist on doing it anyway, tell me—what do you want me to do?"

Mama kissed my father on the cheek. "This is my plan," she started, seconds before the timer went off that signaled that the bread pudding was ready to be taken out of the oven.

It took several hours to get Mama's plan operational. Mama called Susy Mets and got her to agree to participate in the ruse. It was about ten o'clock when people had been moved, the phone call to the killer had been made, and we pulled up in front of the small house. The moon rose, only a sliver less full than it had been the night before. A dog barked from the woods on the right, and a second dog picked up the cry.

The heat from the night felt like a suffocating blanket. I couldn't help but wonder—what if the killer didn't come? What if he was smart enough to slip past Rick and Abe? I wanted to share my doubts with Mama but decided against it; she had enough to worry about already.

We were inside where a ceiling fan sent warm air throughout the living room. Mama looked around, then picked her spot. It was an upholstered chair next to the window, one of two windows that, in the daytime, looked out onto the front porch, the yard, and the road beyond. But now the shades were drawn.

My father shook his head as if he couldn't believe he was going along with this, then he crouched behind Mama's chair, within arm's reach of her body.

I had been instructed to find the light switch to the front porch and be ready to turn it on. I took a deep breath, and crouched down on the floor directly in front of the switch. It was an awkward position, one that had me sitting with my back against a wall ready to spring up like a frog at the sound of Abe's or Rick's voice. "Suppose he doesn't come," I whispered, forgetting my earlier inclination not to throw water on Mama's fire by sharing my doubts.

"He'll be here," she whispered back impatiently. "Now don't say another word!"

Abe and Rick were out there, supposedly hiding within a few yards of wherever the killer chose to take a swipe at Mama. Cliff was behind the sofa. He had come out of his comatose posture of not believing what Mama was going to do, and had agreed to accompany us. I was trying to figure what he could do to save Mama from behind the couch.

The stillness was punctuated by another dog's bark. Mama sat straight up in the chair. The light from a small lamp threw the shadow of her silhouette against the window shade, giving the killer a clear target.

I sat, wondering how long we'd have to wait before things started to pop. A squirrelly feeling in the pit of my stomach started when I began to imagine the killer slithering behind a tree, the moonlight revealing the sinister look in his eyes. I strained to listen for the sound of a twig breaking, a leaf rustling, but the only sound was my heartbeat.

I drew my knees tight against my body and held my breath. My imagination started up again: In my mind's eye I could see the killer wipe his mouth, then move closer to his prey—my mother!

Nervously I put my finger to my mouth, as if to remind myself to keep quiet. Again I began to imagine the killer, to see his lips pulled back tight in a half-crazed smile as he eased up to the uneven stone steps that led to the front porch. I swallowed hard past the lump in my throat.

I imagined the killer lifting his gun and aiming it at Mama's head. My imagination became reality when I heard Abe's voice. "Put it down easy and nobody will get hurt!"

My heart pounded like a drum. Drops of sweat rolled down my face. I swear the next thing I heard was the killer's finger tightening on the trigger.

I jumped up and switched on the porch light.

My father pulled Mama to the floor.

A bullet zinged through the room and lodged in the wall above the sofa.

Mama wasn't hurt, and Herman Spikes would never kill again.

CHAPTER
TWENTY-TWO

"'I have occasionally had the exquisite thrill of putting my finger on a little capsule of truth, and heard it give the faint squeak of mortality under my pressure,' said E. B. White," Mama said, smiling.

We were in the Otis Community Center putting the last-minute touches on the decorations twenty minutes before the guests were due to arrive. Yasmine, Ernest, Rodney, Will, Stacey (Will's "special lady"), Cliff, my father, and I had stopped working. We were all listening to Mama tell how she had figured out that Herman Spikes had killed his wife. Daddy and Cliff and I had heard it before, of course, but we were enjoying hearing Mama tell it again.

"I touched a little capsule of truth when, as I listened to Sarah's story and looked at the scarf around her neck I realized that the cloth Simone had wrapped Sparkle, Curtis and Mack's cat up in, was identical to a red and brown scarf I'd seen in Ruby's bathroom floor in a pile of discarded clothes," she told them. "Jeff Golick, the manager of the Avondale Inn, told us that Ruby wore a reddish brown scarf the night she checked in. Inez Moore told me that the plant manager at the garment factory allowed every employee to take two scarves from each lot. I asked myself, how did Ruby's scarf get to Betty Jo Mets's house? Simone picked up the soiled and wrinkled scarf from Betty Jo's house thinking it was a piece of rag.

"Sarah's story of how she'd spotted Laura Manning's killer because he'd picked up a special pen made me wonder whether or not Ruby's killer picked up her scarf to wipe his fingerprints from the gun and the room. Suppose he took it away with him but then left it at a place where he stashed the money. Suppose he didn't realize what he'd done until he saw Simone bring it out of Betty Jo's house and wrap poor little Sparkle in it."

"And," I interrupted, "he might have shot at you to draw me away from the car so that he could get the scarf back."

"Exactly," Mama said.

"What?" My father asked. "Herman Spikes had shot at you once before?"

Uh-oh, here we go, I thought. We'd managed until now to keep him in the dark about that.

"We didn't know it was Herman at the time," Mama told him.

I wasn't about to mention the hood flying up on

the Honda. I knew my father's blood pressure was already going up. There was no reason to upset him further by telling him we suspected Herman had released the latch on the Honda and that Herman might have bumped us and sent us flying into the ditch. We couldn't prove it anyway.

Mama continued. "Then there were the brand new twenty-dollar bills that Betty Jo gave her boys. Where did she get the money from? Now, I knew Betty Jo very well. She had low morals but she was neither a thief nor a liar. Then I remembered our last conversation the night before her death. She told me she was confused by something, and she asked me to meet her at Portia Bolton's house. I assumed she wanted to ask me something about the care of Curtis and Mack. But when I started thinking about it, I remembered Susy, Betty Jo's cousin, telling me Betty Jo had mentioned having a dream that seemed so real. She told me she stopped talking about the dream when Herman walked up, and that Betty Jo moved into his house right around then.

"Suppose, I continued thinking, that Betty Jo Mets fell asleep after she and Herman had sex at the Otis Motel. Suppose Herman slipped out, went to Avondale, killed Ruby, stole her money, and stopped by Betty Jo's house, which is located between Avondale and Otis, to stash the money for the time being. Suppose, as he slipped back into the motel room, Betty Jo roused and he quieted her, telling her that she was dreaming."

"Then Herman killed Betty Jo?" Will asked.

"Yes," Mama answered. "The truth will come out in the trial, but once I'd talked to Inez Moore and let it out that Ruby might have been murdered, Herman started becoming uncomfortable. I think he overheard Betty Jo talking to me on the phone and decided she wasn't going to be as good of an alibi as he'd first thought."

"He suffocated her like he'd done Ruby," I interjected.

"Problem is, he didn't have time to make it look like she'd killed herself, so he pretended that she died in her sleep," Mama said.

"He didn't know that the autopsy would show that she'd been killed," I said.

"No," Mama admitted. "Still, I had to come up with a way of catching him trying to murder again. It would have to be something that linked him with Ruby and Betty Jo. I decided that link was Betty Jo's concern about a dream that she thought might have been real."

"So after Mama convinced us to let her sit as bait, she called Susy Mets," I said.

"Susy agreed to call Herman and tell him that she'd been thinking about the dream that Betty Jo had mentioned to her," Mama explained.

"Of course, Mama had Susy add a bit more to the conversation that she'd had with her cousin than actually took place," I said.

"It was the only way to get Herman to react," Mama said.

"What did you tell Susy to say?" Ernest asked.

"I asked her to tell Herman that Betty Jo had told her that she saw him come into the motel room sometime after midnight but that Herman had told her she'd been dreaming. Susy assured Herman that she hadn't told anybody what Betty Jo had told her but said that she was thinking about mentioning it to Abe the next morning."

"Then you sat in the chair and waited for Herman to try to kill you?" Rodney asked Mama.

"I couldn't put poor Susy into that position, now could I?"

"Your mama had to be the hero!" Daddy chided.

Mama smiled at my father. "No, James, you were the hero. You pulled me out of the line of Herman's fire, remember."

Daddy nodded, but he wasn't flattered.

"Why did Herman kill Ruby and try to make it look like she'd killed herself?" Rodney asked.

"Inez Moore and Leman made it clear that Herman was being laughed at because of Ruby's extramarital affair. No doubt Herman found out that Ruby had a large sum of money and confronted her. She probably told him she was going to leave him. The thought of her leaving him for Leman with all that money was too much for him.

"Why he decided to kill her in the motel room, I don't know," Mama admitted. "What I think happened is that he secured the room at the Otis Motel for him and Betty Jo before he went home from work.

"Once at home, he started a fight with Ruby, no

doubt hitting her and telling her to get out. Ruby pulled together a few things and left. The only place she had to go was the Avondale Inn, since Leman had already told her that he was ready to end their relationship.

"Herman followed her and, at a safe distance, saw which room she went into. Then he came back to Otis and made plans to spend the night with Betty Jo."

"Why was Leman Moody following you and Simone?" Yasmine asked.

"Leman wasn't following us. It's true he thought that he was suspected of killing Ruby for her money. But he just happened to be passing by when Simone and I came out from Betty Jo's place after Sparkle was taken from our car. Simone called Abe from Atlanta and told him that she thought Leman was the one who had shot at us. Abe pulled Leman in and told him that if anything else happened to us, he'd be the first person questioned. Leman stayed away from Otis and Avondale until after Herman was caught."

"And Inez—what happened to her and her old man?" Will asked.

"They're going to trial soon for stealing from the plant," Mama told him.

"The rapist, Honey Man, had nothing to do with Ruby's murder?" Stacey asked.

"Nothing at all," Mama said. "But I'm glad he was caught."

"The chase is over," I said, ready for a festive

spirit to take hold. "Let's get into the best thirty-fifth wedding anniversary party this town has ever seen!"

My father didn't need any further encouragement: he reached out and pulled Mama into his arms, her jade dress swirling around her ankles. Together they took a few dance steps across the floor. He kissed her lightly on the lips. "Candi and I are going to really do it up tonight," he said proudly.

Mama's body was relaxed; she swayed to imagined music. Now that she had solved the latest mystery in Otis, she was ready to concentrate on their celebration. "Yes, James honey," she agreed happily, "we're really going to do it up tonight!"

We applauded.

And Mama smiled.

If you enjoyed Nora DeLoach's

Mama Pursues Murderous Shadows

*you won't want to miss any
of the tantalizing mysteries
in this series!*

*Look for the newest
adventure featuring Candi
and Simone Covington,*

Mama Cracks a Mask of Innocence

*at your favorite bookseller's
in spring 2001.*

ABOUT THE AUTHOR

NORA DELOACH is an Orlando, Florida, native presently living in Decatur, Georgia. She is married and the mother of three. Her novels include four previous Mama mysteries. She is at work on her sixth, *Mama Cracks a Mask of Innocence*.